I0788413

Sign up at pgshriver.com now to receive free books and updates on new books.

Delaying Eternity

P.G. SHRIVER

Acknowledgements

A special thanks to my family for giving me the uninterrupted time to write this novel and the encouragement to continue working on it until the deadline. Without their support, I would not be a writer because I would have to support myself.

Dedication

For anyone who never has been, but someday will be, in love for eternity

And for everyone who already is

MEL

My eyes squeezed shut during the spin; I pried them open.

Shooting pain brought a flash of blinks.

I should have kept them closed, because now I'll always have that image of my mother embedded in my mind.

A web of red criss-crossed her face.

I recalled one of my science teachers explaining that blood wasn't red until it was introduced to oxygen.

The thick, sticky, warm feeling of my mother's body juice where it touched my cheek nauseated me.

What really concerned me, right before my world went dark, wasn't the blood. I could tolerate seeing blood. It was the proximity of my body to my mother's. No worries about my own dripping, broken, scentless nose filled my thoughts. Since I was a child, I couldn't stand being this close to my mother; whenever she touched me, my skin crawled.

A painful shift of my pupils showed me that her eyes moved beneath lightly closed lids. She inhaled, exhaled; I felt it on my chin over the pain. So, she was only unconscious. I could live with that. She had spent most of our quality time that way.

Still, tiny bugs swept across my skin.

I felt like one of those olives in the jar, the green ones that she sometimes put in her martinis, our bodies squeezed so tightly a fork couldn't pull us free.

The biting odor of her vodka breath seeped into my open mouth. Instinctively, the taste crinkled my nose. A small cry of pain escaped my lips.

Too late to change my mind, the pain assailed me.

The last mental picture before darkness descended on me was Mom and I swimming around in a giant martini glass, pinned together by a toothpick. I think a chuckle even crept up my throat.

Darkness.

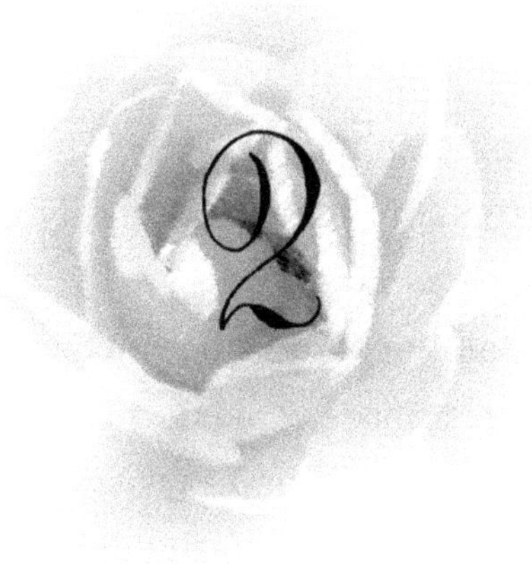

$When$ light fought back the gray behind my lids, my eyes opened to ceiling tiles, bright lights and floating heads speaking an incoherent language. I couldn't move my head. People hovered. Darkness crept at the edge of my vision, weaving in and around the talking heads; I let it consume them and take me back to oblivion.

The prickling of light speckled my shaded lids again, so I worked the heaviness out of the thick blinds and forced them open. My head moved freely this time. Ugly green walls, pale yellow light, and that ceiling full of tiles told me I was in a hospital room, not to mention the antiseptic smell.

No pain pierced when I blinked or crinkled or moved.

Thank you pain meds.

No doctors or nurses or family bordered my bed.

This certainly couldn't be how Sleeping Beauty felt after her prince awakened her, and she slept much longer than I had. Of course, something crucial to that plan was missing: my prince.

Muffled voices drifted in from the hallway through the sliver of opening in my door. When I focused my attention on them, I could hear the speech as clear as if it were happening next to my bed.

"No… no… the mother's right here in this room. No… she didn't make it. No…"

My eardrums closed. "What? My mother's dead?" I mouthed. They were talking about *my* mother. A whirlpool of emotions twisted my heart.

The part of me that loved her wanted to let loose a scream of mourning.

The part of me that hated her wanted to plant my feet on the bed and jump up and down.

I read somewhere drunk drivers in most cases survived car accidents, while their passengers died.

I became aware of a warm, dampness sliding down my cheek as the pieces of the morning I ended up here sifted through my memory:

"Mother! Slow down! The school's only eight blocks away!" Tidy white houses with manicured lawns, leaving trees, and various street signs blurred the corner of my vision as my words of warning rushed out in one breath.

"I'm not worried about you being late! I can't be late!" She shot the stupid look at me. I hate when she does that! The raised brows, the head jerk in my direction, and the half snarl really made me feel the way she intended. Anger burst forth followed by a hot lava of words.

"Well... if you wouldn't stay up so late drink..." As angry as her stupid look made me, I stopped the flow of ugly words.

I was so tired of fighting all the time!

Just keep your mouth shut until you get to school! Then you can complain to your best friends.

"What are you saying Miss-Know-It-All? I'm a drunk?" She turned her twisted, angry face towards

me.

Her olive tinted iris' spewed pimento veins toward the corners and met mine, the wrinkles around them slightly smoothing. Below those bloodshot eyes, dark circles formed, small half moons of abuse. She looked so old.

Behind that haggard face, I saw it.

Through the driver's side window, it barreled toward us.

The glance over my shoulder confirmed that my mother had just sped through a two way stop.

The impact of the dump truck careened my nose into my mother's shoulder.

The first rotation of the car cracked my head into the passenger window.

The car spun.

My brain swam against it.

The spinning seemed to go on forever.

Nausea filled my empty stomach.

Wordlessly, I begged the car to stop.

Finally, a telephone pole drew the car to it like a magnet and smashed us to a stop. Because the dump truck clobbered the left side, and the telephone pole bent the right side, I was closer to my mother than I had been in years, closer than I ever wanted to be.

The hospital no longer had a reason to hold me hostage. I turned eighteen in December, so there was no need to seek out social services or my addict father to sign me out, not like they could find him.

I watched through the open door of the room as a doctor plucked my chart, flipped to the last page, signed off, and then I left. As I had learned in Driver's Ed, the car insurance picked up the hospital tab.

While I exited, the hospital doors opened to a pregnant woman in a wheel chair, her husband in a panic beside her, and I slipped by them...alone. The image of the new family made me cry, their happiness evident. How very different from the day I was born, I assured myself.

A black Hearst awaited me. I ducked into the gloomy silence filling the front seat; the funeral home driver glanced in the mirror at my mother's body tucked away in a black bag in the back. His dark hair and somber features fit the role. I wondered what Ruthie would do if she met him.

The driver shivered.

He must be new to the job. For some deeply satisfying reason, that thought made me smile.

Why would you work for a funeral home if you freaked out over dead bodies?

The funeral home loomed before us, and the driver pulled up under the archway where two guys met us to remove the black bag in the back.

I don't remember talking about the preparations. The funeral home's morbidity brought battle to my heart; my tears lost. Certain the receptionist didn't understand my lack of emotion during this tragic event, I smiled broadly at her on my way out the door; her expression didn't change. *What a horrible place to work*, I thought, unless you could creep out the new people.

The driver dropped me off at home on his way back to the hospital; no body filled the space in the back this time. I assured him I could walk the three blocks home, but he wouldn't listen. As the Hearst rolled to a stop in front of my house, I opened the door. The car hadn't stopped completely and I flinched awaiting Mom's slap. She must have loved me to an extent if she didn't want me falling out of a moving vehicle to get squished by the tires, yet not, if she would risk my life by drinking and driving.

There was no slap.

The driver pulled two potted plants from the back and placed them on the porch, then silently walked away. I thanked him for the ride, but he just shook his head. Those people were always so quiet. I couldn't understand that. I mean, you're not going to scare the dead by talking loudly, right?

Respect, I guessed.

Sadness swept over me as his solemn figure drove away in the black vehicle. I would have taken a cab, but I had no choice. I didn't have any money. There never was any money in the house. It always went to booze. Even the Bank of Mel, where safety deposit boxes held socks and underwear, was broke. No matter what clever place I hid babysitting money, or birthday money, the magic house chewed it, swallowed it and spit it back out into a new full glass bottle, capped it, and left it on the counter for Mom. I was slightly curious that Grandma and Grandpa hadn't picked me up, but then, that's why they call it "estranged".

Dawning crashed like that dump truck into my mind: I had no money at all! How was I going to live and finish my senior year?

I couldn't drop out; I was so close to finishing. I

was at the top of the class! I had worked so hard to escape to college and live my own life away from my mother! Now what?

During my lonely years in middle school, I would have jumped at the chance to walk away from school and never return, but then school had been a bullied struggle. It was always difficult for people my age to accept me. Since we moved here, though, last summer, and I started attending Parkville High, I had actually made friends I could talk to on my level without being judged. They understood me, spoke my language. We seldom had disagreements.

We were our own little clique this year, although each of us was very different from the others, and all of us would have accepted anyone else into our little group. Everywhere we went, we had a blast! A devious smile crossed my lips as I recalled last weekend at the mall... guy watching.

Ruthie didn't have a shy bone in her body, hooting and whistling, calling after guys of all sorts, flirting shamelessly, casting about her flaming red hair, batting her green hazel eyes—the liberated one.

Mags had the best figure, the largest bust, and glistening black hair, green highlights overlaying the darkness. A hint of coy mischief tinged her dark brown eyes. The guys acted toward her the way Ruthie did toward them, without the hair moves. Mags wasn't the forceful type, but the most experienced at dating.

Kathy never knew what to say, the shy, quiet type, but somehow she attracted guys like a magnet with her up to date fashions, aloof personality and bashful smile. Her chin length, golden brown layers swung about her face when she shook her head at Ruthie's antics. Kath was the oldest, and my best friend of the three, though I would never share that information with Ruthie and Mags.

And me, I just went along for the fun. I wasn't interested and neither were the guys. I knew I wasn't ugly, and I had some personality, a dry sense of humor, intellect, otherwise, my three crazy friends would have ditched me three and a half years ago when we moved here. Endlessly, Ruthie and Mags tried to change my looks, set me up, make me more interested in guys, but Kath always made them back down, "Knock it off you two! There's nothing about Mel that needs changing. She's great the way she is!"

If I were a guy, I'd be all up in Kathy's business. She understood me and appreciated my driven personality. Of course, it made a difference that she was the only one of the three who had actually seen my mother at her worst! She was the only one who had witnessed Mother's cruelty and neglect first hand.

Last weekend at the mall, after we caught the attention of a group of guys hanging out, Ruthie suggested a detour to Victoria Secret. Kathy's face lit bright red. I'm pretty sure mine showed a little pink, too. "Let's go!" Mags nodded. Of course, the guys held back in the hallway as we entered the store, passing looks between them, curiosity playing over their faces.

Intuition told me that when we left the store, we would hit the food court with these guys, especially with Mags and Ruthie flashing bright colored, lacy undergarments at them for approval, or holding matching sets of bras and panties against their bodies and prancing about in front of the doors. And I would have to turn down, or not, one of them. I never dated, but that was because it was never a top priority for me. I figured it could wait. I was finally happy in school. I had friends to have fun with, and I was going to college on scholarships! Somehow I felt that guys would only mess that up for me.

Mom, on the other hand, believed I should

date, party, have fun! She never understood the other reason I didn't date. It couldn't be that I didn't want the embarrassment of bringing a guy home to meet *her*. It couldn't be that I didn't trust my own emotions because she screwed with them all the time! It couldn't be that I was afraid if I did bring a guy home, she would embarrass me by making a move on him.

"This would look great on you, Mel!" Ruthie held a matching set against my slender body.

"You should totally buy that!" Mags's eyes widened.

"I couldn't. Really, it's not me."

"It is so totally you! I'm coming back to get it for you!"

"Mags . . ." Kathy rolled her eyes at Mags.

"Oh, hush! I am."

I sighed. Sometimes Mags overpowered us both. So that's how I obtained my first Victoria Secret undergarments that I never got a chance to wear, because my mother found the bag in my room while searching for money, and as we were the same size, the bag disappeared.

Before we left Victoria Secret, Mags hit the sample perfume and doused us in her favorite scents.

"Hey," the tall, rock hard, overconfident guy called to Mags as we exited the store. Boy, was he in trouble. Mags hated that type of guy, but the cat liked to play with the mice before leaving them broken on the floor. Yeah, Mags was the cat.

"Hey," Mags countered, sizing him up.

"You wanna grab some pizza?"

Mags searched our eyes; we were going anyway. Dinner and a show, I thought. We all loved to watch Mags at work with those annoying ego filled guys. She was a sight to behold, and we were an enraptured audience.

"Sure," she flashed her perfect white teeth, bounced her eyebrows, and turned, clearly the leader of this pack of eight. It wasn't long before Mr. Ego vied for leadership, though. Mags was not about to let that happen.

And naturally, before we parted ways, the shyest of the four guys choked out the question I always dread, "So, uhm, can I call you?"

We hadn't said more than two words to each other all night. "Uh...no! I don't date." I sighed. It wasn't a lie like Mags was telling Mr. Ego this very moment, Ruthie and Kath sharing knowing looks with each other, having both turned down the two that had been talking to them.

It had been a really fun night, though!

Remembering that night brought worry; how would I stay in school?

Was I going to have to move from our rental house...move away from Parkville...quit school?

My next thought was of life insurance.

Surely Mom had life insurance through work!

These thoughts occupied my mind while I dug around in my book bag, cringing at the dried blood speckling it, and pulled out the spare house key.

As I unlocked the front door, I noticed several bouquets of flowers, pink and white carnations, yellow daisies, and various brightly colored chrysanthemums lying about the porch next to the potted plants.

I pushed my key in the lock and turned my hand.

The door squeaked open.

The house was as we left it the morning of the accident. Clean, except for the coffee mug and cheap vodka on the kitchen table. In our relationship, I was the OCD clean one; mom was the slob.

I dropped my bag next to the kitchen door, picked up the bottle and mug, and tossed them both in the trash. One glance around the kitchen and I decided there was no dire need I could fill here. I hefted my book bag to my room, deposited it on my second hand desk chair, and belly flopped onto my bed.

The wooden headboard thumped the wall.

That night, I cried myself to sleep for the first time since I had awakened from a nightmare at the age of six, slipped into my parents' room, and searched the entire house, before realizing they had left me alone and gone out.

The next few days blurred with my tears. I didn't know where they were coming from, the tears. I didn't understand my mourning. Maybe it was just loneliness. More like, I was having emotional withdrawals from the verbal abuse, neglect, smell of alcohol. I'd always been alone, pretty much. Funny how the loss of a loved one, even though she had been lost years ago, the idea of being completely alone, though my entire life had been spent that way, affected me.

More flowers appeared outside our house,

strangers in mourning, rubberneckers of the accident, neighbors who pitied our situation. I kept thinking: if they had really known her…

Mother hadn't wanted a service of any kind when she 'moved on', as she would say. She always told me she wanted to be cremated. Of course, she usually said this in a drunken state, so I was slightly shocked when I realized she got what she wanted, because somebody planted a small urn on the mantle in front of the mirror, probably my invisible Grandma and Grandpa.

Grandma and Grandpa came by the house a couple of times during my first few days following the accident. They left notes scrawled in seventy-year-old chicken scratch. Grandma taught school before she retired. I always thought her handwriting should be neater.

I suppose I had gone for a walk or was taking a nap when they stopped. I spent a lot of time walking around, wondering what I was going to do. Grandma and Grandpa never had the time to visit, just snoop. As a matter of fact, I hadn't seen them in years. They always seemed to visit Mom when I wasn't home.

And they always signed their notes, Lester and

Paula in that old person scratch. Mom always called them by their first names. I began to wonder if they really were my grandparents.

The note said they had brought a bag of groceries, comfort food. Flipping the light switch and opening the door, I searched the pantry for new items: packages of chocolate chip cookies, boxes of brownies, Mac and Cheese.

A cold steam brushed my face as I opened the freezer and found my favorite ice cream, Rocky Road. Realizing their invisible visit made me feel a little better, I crumpled the note like Mom always did, and went to take a nap. I suppose my grandparents loved me in their own freaky way, even though it seemed that they never really wanted to be grandparents. Heck, I don't think they had wanted to be parents. The way Mom drank, I would bet on that.

Another Monday crept up on me and my body felt drained. I was tired of crying, worrying, sleeping and walking. A more positive approach filled my thoughts: everything would work out fine. That was my lifelong motto. Hiding behind couches, under beds, in closets, trying to stay away from the strange men my mother brought home:

Everything will work out fine!

I decided to return to school. Enough moping around the house, moping wasn't going to help my situation, cure the loneliness. I had to do something, and school was that something that I needed to do.

A familiar car horn blasted outside my front door. Our totaled car now resided at the residence of totaled cars, wherever that was, so I was certain Kath waited at the curb.

I wondered why I hadn't seen Kathy since the accident. As a matter of fact, I hadn't seen any of my friends. Most likely, I missed them because I was sleeping so hard when they stopped. It wasn't like we hung out every day after school or anything. There was so little time with school and part time jobs and extracurricular activities. Once in a while, we all met at the mall, or the movies, or the bowling alley, but usually...She probably had stopped and honked every morning since I got out of the hospital, but I was too out of it to hear her horn or care to return to life.

Oh, well, I reached for my book bag in my chair and discovered a brand new one, no dried blood, and it just happened to be the one I wanted for

Christmas with my college choice logo on it. The one I never received from Mom, because, of course, the brandy for the eggnog took precedence. Hmm...Grandma and Grandpa apparently had transferred all of my books and emergency items into it. Seeing it, thinking of my absent grandparents doing something so nice for me, perked me up.

The morning sun twinkled about the house through late winter branches as I locked the door. The warmth reached out to me, embracing the cold emptiness within. It even made me smile, in a sad way. I wished my mom and I had been closer, more in tune with each other. I wished she would have enjoyed mornings like this. I wished she could have enjoyed any morning without having to drink first. A vision of an early morning jog with Mom ran through my thoughts as I stepped into the street behind Kath's car.

My watch ticked away the minutes and told me we were going to be late. I always worried about being late, and usually we never were. Kath didn't say anything when I climbed in the car. She looked sadder than me, making it a short, silent trip.

The second warning bell echoed through the

hallway as we moved from bright morning sun to dim, fluorescent light. I found myself in a funk again. Maybe I wasn't really ready for this.

At our lockers, I saw Kathy glance in my direction, but she didn't smile. I hoped she would be happy I was back, help me get back in the swing, catch me up on classes, but I guess seeing me would make all three of them sad for me.

"Hey," I touched her arm, then reached up to twist the dial on my lock. It was stuck, as usual. I jerked on it, without success. I didn't try again. I leaned my head into the vented metal door with a thunk. Is this how it would be from now on?

"I am so sorry, Mel. I stopped by Thursday, but…" Kath shook her head. Tears filled her eyes.

"What? Hey, Kath, don't do that. It's okay. I'm okay. Everything will work out fine! Don't cry. I'm more concerned with where I'm going to stay now. I don't have any money that I know of, unless my elusive grandparents are picking up the tab for my life." I comforted her with a gentle stroke over her bare arm. Me comforting her…oh, well, that was our relationship: me, the stronger of the two; Kath, the sensitive one. No change here. Her forehead pressed against her locker door, she peered toward my locker from the corner of her eye.

"I asked my parents if you could live with us. I'd been bugging them, because of your mom, you know. I didn't want to tell you. I was going to surprise you if they said yes." I barely heard the whispered words. "I guess that's not necessary now," she shrugged.

Wow! I had no idea she was up to that! Excitement bubbled within me. That would be awesome!

"They finally said yes." She forced a wispy smile, but her depression soon wiped it away. Maybe that's another reason she was so sad, because I didn't need to move in with her now.

She was such a drama queen, always overplaying the bad situations, and deemphasizing the good! I rolled my eyes in her direction, a huge smile brightening my spirits, hoping to bring her mood up.

WHAM!

My knees went weak!

Just like I always read in those mushy romance novels Ruthie passed on to me that I have a secret passion for!

Love at first sight!

A new guy... a hot, new guy, glided into my view, and just as quickly disappeared behind a row of gray lockers down the adjoining hall.

One glimpse of gorgeousness took over my entire brain. Kath's depression dissipated. His incredible image burned into my mind: dark brown mussy hair, rosy chiseled cheeks, long and not too lean and the coolest retro black leather jacket I'd ever seen!

Those few steps he took crossing the intersection replayed in my mind like a fantastic football highlight on television; yes, football is another secret passion.

Why had I never noticed him before? He had to be new!

"Hey, Kath, who... was... that?" I whispered in her direction, but Ruthie and Mags bounded over from the girl's room, cutting off her chance to answer me when their widened eyes took us in.

Kathy's overdramatic tears could always bring us running.

Ruth and Mags enveloped her in a hug.

I was too curious about Mr. Hottie to join them. Determined to see him again, I took a couple of steps down the hall. The thought crossed my mind to skip first period and peek in every classroom until I found him.

Never had I seen a guy that aroused my interest so much. Usually, I kept my distance pretty well. This was definitely unfamiliar ground for me. I bit my lower lip with reasoning, but not for long; obsessive love chased out the doubt.

Instead of Kathy, I would envelope him, run down the halls shouting his name...if I knew his name.

Mr. Keeter, the Social Studies teacher stepped out in the hall to gather stragglers. "Ladies, I know you have suffered a tragic experience, but life goes on and class has already begun! Let's move along now."

I didn't even remember following the girls to class, but I had to focus. I'd worked too hard to graduate at the top of my class to slack off now because of some Greek god. Besides, if he was here, in school, I would run into him again.

Guilt inundated my curiosity. Was it wrong for me to feel like this so soon after...

Nah. This is what my hard to please mother had always wanted for me. She would be thrilled!

This new feeling was so odd. I have had many

loves: strays that I took in as a pet, until Mother discovered they cost too much and interfered with her habit; romance novels, most recently for adults; football, which I watched as often as I could afford, never missing a home game; old movies like Love Story and Alfred Hitchcock thrillers; I could go on. But I had never fallen in love with a guy before.

I'd even one time wondered if I was a lesbian, but I didn't have feelings for girls, either.

Suddenly, I was overpowered with a need to know this guy. Did my mother's death awaken some buried emotions within me? The sunlight twinkled upon the freshly cleaned window beside me, a maybe yes answer? Maybe it was the concussion? Maybe I was just lonelier than before? Perhaps, like the cliché, a near death experience made me want to live. The sun definitely seemed to sparkle more.

I went through the rest of the day with my head in the clouds; a slow boil determination built that plotted and planned within the loops, twists and turns of my roller coaster emotions just how to make that guy mine. Of course, I needed to meet him first!

That could be the difficult part. Though my friends have tried repeatedly over the past year to hook me up with some guy or another, I just never had any interest— until now.

It concerned me that most guys didn't approach me to ask me out, either, so I had concluded that they most likely thought I was a snob, or they were intimidated by my intelligence, if they knew me, which was even more likely. Then there was the grapevine. I'm sure my repeated turn downs had earned me a reputation of rejection. Why had I done that? I think, actually, that I just didn't want to put myself out there to get hurt.

Besides that how could I ever bring a date home to Mom? I was sure he would introduce himself and receive the stupid look in reply! Or even worse, she would steal him away like my Victoria Secret undergarments.

I know I'm not the best-looking girl in the school. I mean, I guess I don't look bad, but only the best could get that guy's attention!

My head, cupped comfortably in my hands, nodded reflexively and continuously as I day dreamed and pondered. Fortunately, the teacher hadn't called on me to answer a question.

Looking down at my faded hand me down shirt — Mags had given it to me; and my ripped jeans – "They're supposed to be that way!" Kath smiled at me— I definitely needed to do some work on my appearance. My hand drifted to my long, brown hair not so neatly pulled back into a ponytail bun, loose strands hanging down around my face and poking out at odd angles in back. Seriously! How long have I had this bun in my hair? Since the beginning of time? I couldn't recall a time when I'd done my hair differently, even when we went to the mall! This morning I had awakened with it in my hair, sort of fingered through the strands about my face and left!

Geeez! I didn't recall ever thinking about my appearance in my entire high school career! I glanced around at the girls in class. As if my soul awakened from a deep centuries long sleep, I viewed their modern makeup, hardly visible yet complimenting, their clothes and accessories, piercings and nails, all modern looks. I flushed, feeling somewhat like a cavewoman.

Where have I been?

I needed some desperate change!

My quick thinking brain shouted, MALL TRIP!

Get the girls on it! That's what they've been waiting for!

Ruthie always wore her makeup just perfect; I've always packaged as is. I have great skin, though. What would a little makeup hurt? And I do tie up my hair, but…

Mags always put her hair together well. Maybe she could help me with that. She had those awesome green highlights that I've admired ever since she came to school with them. They looked really cool in her long dark layers! When she pulled it up into a ponytail, the green streaks really popped all over the place!

Sure, that's what I'll do!

He'll notice me, then!

I mean, I don't know about the green, but maybe a new cut and style, new clothes…

Dollar signs flashed before my eyes!

And just where would I get the money for all of that? Ask grandma and grandpa? Not likely, though I did think about leaving a note for them. Ha ha! In chicken scratch! It might be weeks before they stopped by again, though.

I needed a babysitting job or two!

My mind stayed on him the rest of the day, even

through the mall trip the girls planned at lunch.

34

DAVIS

"*Give* it a little gas!" I yelled over the roaring motor.

"What?" my dorky sister yelled back.

"Gas! More gas!" I wound my index finger in a circle as I peered around the hood at her.

"Oh, okay!"

Vrooooom!

That motor was piano music to a troubled ape. "That's good! Kill it!"

The motor quieted, and I reached in to tweak the carb one more turn.

"Let me go with you, Davis, please?" Donna jumped up and down next to me.

"No! I told you, if we both disappear, Mom and Dad will know something's up. Dad would kill me if he found out I was still going after that lecture he gave me." I wiped my hands on the greased up rag from my back pocket. Then I reached up and slammed the hood.

"I'll tell them I'm staying with a friend. Come on, Davis!"

I ran my hand down the side of my red '57 Chevy. She was a beauty. Red body, white top, wide white wall tires, and a motor I'd built up to beat anything on the streets. I'd saved my money, all of it, and worked my butt off for the last six years to earn enough to buy her. She was the hottest used car on the block, in perfect condition. Sweet, unblemished bench seats, clean, unscathed body, perfectly pointed tail fins, and best of all, she was all mine, free and clear! She and I were going to conquer it all in college, and win every race that came our way.

But I had to focus on tonight, the big race that would crown me the County Champion. Word was spreading. I had made enough money from racing her to pay for my first two years of college.

"Come on, Davis!" my annoying sister butted in on my buzz. If it hadn't been for her, I wouldn't even have to make money for college! My hand rested on the tail fin, the feel of the polishing rag between the metal and my fingers. Donna's light sorrel ponytail flipped as she bounced in front of me, still begging. People we met found it difficult to believe we were twins, and both going off to college at the same time.

"Donna, I told you, no! If Mom and Dad find out…" I stared her down. I'd managed to make that money racing without their knowledge, until Dad had caught me recently. That conversation did not go well.

"If Mom and Dad find out about what?" a deep voice queried behind me.

"Dad!" Donna and I smiled at him in unison.

"I smell a rat. What's up with you two?" My dad was a big man, six-foot-five and bulging with muscle. He went to college with hopes of pro football, blew out a knee, end of story. He came back from college, without a degree, because he lost his scholarship and his parents couldn't afford to keep him in, went to work in the local steel plant and worked his way up. He did alright by us. We never wanted for anything and we were taught to earn our own way. He had a kind heart and heavy hand.

His big arms crossed, "Well, son?"

"Well...we were just talking about..." I stumbled for a lie.

He would kill me if he knew I was still racing, taking chances like that with the future I had ahead of me.

"We can't tell you, Daddy," Donna slithered up to him, oozing her daddy's little girl charm, and patted his arms.

He turned his eyes to her green ones, "Why not?"

"Well, you and Mom have an anniversary coming up, right?"

"We do?" He asked, dropping his arms to his sides.

"Yes, Daddy! In two weeks!"

Dad cut his eyes to the neatly manicured lawn,

then turned his head toward the house, "Yes, yes, I think you're right. You know, I got something to take care of. Son, you got that car lookin' tip-top! Proud of you!" he growled over his shoulder as he went toward the house.

"Donna, you always have a wild card." I shook my head.

"Well, that one was easy. I knew Dad had forgotten their anniversary. Betcha he's getting his keys and leaving for town in about thirty minutes?"

"Nah, he'll wait 'til he gets off work Monday." I rubbed at a handprint.

"I'll bet not. If he leaves in a while for town, you have to take me tonight."

I knew he wouldn't, so I agreed.

She might be Daddy's girl, but I learned frugality from Dad. He wasn't about to waste the extra gas to go into town today just for an anniversary present for Mom. Not when the Sears and Roebuck was open late and he had two weeks to pick one up. Besides, it would clue Mom in if he left for town today. He never went to town on Saturdays unless she made him go. Sometimes Donna wasn't too bright.

I rubbed on my sweet ride, polishing and

caressing. She was my one true love. I'd focused and worked so hard on my future that I hadn't made time for girls, but I sure had time for her. She was going to take me places. Girls would only take me to one place—the wedding alter. They weren't hookin' me into that. Many had tried, too, but I stayed focused and let them flutter about me trying their best.

As dark fell, Donna dragged her feet outside, "Mom says dinner's ready," she sulked back into the house, ponytail drooping forward over her boney shoulder.

I had been right. Dad never left the house. Nineteen years of knowledge told me he was in there balancing the checkbook and trying to figure out how much he would have left this month to purchase something nice for Mom.

I whistled my way into the house, washed my hands and took my seat at the table.

Mom cooked better than anyone I knew. Shoveling meatloaf and mashed potatoes into my mouth, I realized that when I got married, this is what I wanted. I wanted a marriage just like my parents'. I wanted a nice home with a couple of kids, neither of which I wanted to be like my sister.

She was such a big pain in my neck.

"Slow down, Davis!" Mom scolded. "You'll have digestive problems."

Mom always jumped me about eating too fast. Dad called me the human vacuum cleaner. I couldn't help it. I had things to do.

"I'm in a hurry, Mom. I gotta eat and go pick up Franky and Joanie."

Rrrrrrriiiinnnng! The phone burst through the dinner conversation.

"Don't answer that!" My dad grumbled.

"I got it!" Donna jumped hopefully.

"Donna Louise Wilburn!" Dad's voice boomed.

The ringing stopped, both from the phone and in my ear. I sat to Dad's left, right in the path of the phone.

"Oh, it's you. Yeah... yeah... okay! Shut up, Jerkface!" She slammed down the receiver.

"Donna Louise!" My mother cried, "That is not how a lady talks on the phone."

"Franky?" I asked between bites.

"Yes, the Jerkface! He said they were ready when you were and to pick them up at the park." Donna stuck her tongue out at me.

"You're grounded young lady!" Dad stated

casually, and lifted a spoonful of peas and mashed potatoes to his mouth.

"Dad!" Donna whined.

"You did exactly what I told you not to do! That phone does not get answered during dinner! You're lucky we have a phone at all! When I was your age, we had to tie two tin cans together with string and…" Donna flew from the table and stomped up the stairs, slamming her door for emphasis.

"Honey, couldn't you have waited until after dinner to ground her? She already eats like a bird."

"Sorry, hon. I'll take her a plate up and talk to her in a bit."

"Okay. What do you and Franky have planned tonight, Davis?" Mom turned her smile to me.

"Planned? Huh? Oh, nothing. Maybe a movie, bowling alley. I don't know."

"Well, I was going to ask you to take your sister, I mean, unless you have a date?" Mom's brows rose. I frowned and shook my head at her. "But, that doesn't matter now that she can't go. You three have fun."

Mom looked disappointed. She wanted me to find a girlfriend. It didn't matter how many times I told her that I wasn't ready to date, every time I went out with Franky and Joanie she hoped I would meet someone. Joanie tried to set me up once without telling me or Franky. It didn't go well. She didn't try again.

"Ahh, if it weren't for that girl's temper, she'd have her own boyfriend to take her places," Dad threw in his two cents. At least he understood my situation with Donna. It was bad enough being her twin, but having to tote her around everywhere was worse. It bugged her that I was able to save my money and buy my own car, when she couldn't get past a store window without blowing hers.

"Ahh," Mom started, "if it weren't for her father being such a mean old cuss, she would have a boyfriend to take her places!"

Dad chuckled.

I swiped a roll around my plate to collect the rest of the gravy and grabbed another one for the road, "I gotta run!"

"Wait a minute young man! We're still eating."

"Honey, let 'im go. It won't be long before it's just you and me again. We might as well get used to it now. I'll fix Donna's plate; you take it up and talk to her."

"Rrrr, manners have gone to pot in this house!"

I closed the door on the conversation as Dad teased Mom about finally being alone. I grinned. Yep, when I was ready for it, that was exactly the kind of love I wanted.

Rolling up to the park, I had to admit to myself for the millionth time, Joanie was a real fox. Her long blonde hair trailed behind her as she swung forward on the wooden swing in the park. Chills ran through me when she looked at me with those large, round eyes. I swore if I looked deep enough, I would be able to see dolphins playing in her irises. Franky sure was a lucky guy.

"Come on, Joanie, he's here! We gotta drive all the way to Burkeville for the race!"

"I'm coming! Why do we always have to go to

stupid races? Why can't we do something fun for a change? Let's go to the drive in movie!" she pleaded, batting her long dark eyelashes.

"I told you, this is the last one. My buddy's gonna become King of the County tonight!" Franky grinned at me through the windshield, "Right, buddy?' flash of perfect white teeth through the windshield, two pats on the hood, head sticking through the side window.

Tapping the dash once, I nodded, "She's ready!"

"Hi, Davis," Joanie pouted.

"Hi, Joanie," I looked out the driver's side window.

Feeling that way about my best friend's girl was not right, but there wasn't a guy around that didn't try to take her from Franky. She was a year younger than us, and Franky just played it cool and distant when she brought up other guys hitting on her. That's what kept her around. Guys always wanted to fight for her, and I could see why. Built with a more than perfectly ample body, those pouty pink lips, and innocent baby blues, I would jump over the seat to sit back there with her if not for Franky. I had to keep reminding myself what my future had in store and that I was Franky's best friend.

When other guys drooled over her and came on to her, Franky hadn't had to fight any one of them for her honor. Because she was head over heels for him.

"Hi, Donna!" Joanie perked up when she opened the back door.

I almost broke my neck whipping around to look. Franky peered over the seat as he climbed in, "Hey, Red, whatcha doin' down there?"

"Hey, Joanie. Hey, Jerkface!" Donna hopped up onto the seat.

"Yeah, what are you doing down there? Dad grounded you! You're gonna get both of us in trouble! Man, now I gotta take you home and if I do that, I'll forfeit. I can't afford to miss this one!"

"Oh, Davis, sheez! It's not the first time I climbed out my bedroom window! I'm nineteen years old. He can't ground me anymore!"

"As long as you live there and don't pay rent, yes he can!"

"Not legally!"

"He could kick you out!"

"Not likely!"

"Dang it, Donna! You ruined the whole night!"

"Ah, just take her along. Tell your Dad she stowed away and you didn't know."

Peering out the window into the darkness, one...two...three deep breaths, kept me from ripping her off the backseat and dumping her right there in the park. Man, this night couldn't get more messed up!

"Oh, Donna, look what Franky got me today!" My eyes rolled to Franky catching a light reflection on the way.

"Oh my gosh! Joanie that's beautiful! Davis, look! Is that . . ." Donna's jaw fell open.

"Yep, we're gettin' hitched," Franky's broad smile told Davis it was the real deal. Not like other guys just trying to get something in return for a little jewelry.

"Tell your mom and dad, man?" I was happy for him, but a little sad, too. He was giving in to the norm.

"Oh, yah! They're really excited!"

"Congratulations!" I stuck my hand out for a firm handshake. I really was excited for him and Joanie.

"Have you set a date? Jerkface is getting married! I can't believe it!"

The way Donna rambled on about it, anyone would have thought it was her getting married. Wave after wave of excitement flowing from the backseat caused my anger to vanish. I started the car and pulled away from the park. We had a long drive. I didn't have time to take Donna home. We'd just have to deal with Dad later.

"This news calls for milkshakes for the road! Don't you think, Franky?"

"Depends, who's buying?"

"Your best man!" I threw my half smile his way. Life was changing too fast. Out of high school, off to college, my best friend tying the knot; oh, well, I was going out with a bang! Tonight, everyone around these parts would remember my name! Everyone would talk about Davis Wilburn.

As if reading my mind, Franky patted my shoulder, "One day, I'll be telling my grandkids about this night, the night their Uncle Davis won the County Drag. This is gonna be the best night ever!"

Donna and Joanie bounced in the rearview mirror as I left rubber on the corner of Belling and Vine.

"**Man!** Look at that crowd!" Franky's jaw dropped.

I did. So many kids lined the raceway, funneling between cars, leaning against cars, that my stomach knotted. With this many kids knowing about the race, I wondered how the location could possibly stay a secret.

"Yeah." I parked in the shoulder at a slant facing the road. "I hope we don't get raided. That's a lot of people with secret knowledge."

"Ah, most of them rode out with somebody else,

so they probably didn't know ahead of time. It'll be alright, man!"

"Wow! Look at all those guys!" Donna grinned from ear to ear.

"Yeah, just watch yourself, Donna! You're not even supposed to be here!"

"Oh, don't be a drag!" She stuck her tongue out as she threw open the door. "Come on, Joanie!"

"Franky?" Joanie leaned her face close to my buddy's ear and pouted.

"Sure, go, doll! Just don't forget who you came with."

"Never!" she planted a kiss on his cheek, hopped out of the car, and walked off with my sister to mingle.

I sipped the last of my milkshake as I watched Joanie shake away. "I can't believe you just let that girl float like that! Aren't you worried she won't come back?"

"Nah. We got a sure thing, man!"

"Nothing's for sure, Franky!"

"What? Buddy, there are two things that are certain in this world: you laying a strip on that road tonight, and me and Joanie."

"I don't get it, how you know." I'd asked my dad

the same question once about Mom. How did he know he was in love, really in love? I hadn't found it yet, apparently. I hadn't wasted much time tryin'.

"Well, for one, she loves me and only me. It's just the kinda thing when it happens, you know. And two, she's knocked up."

"Aw, man, Franky! Now what are you gonna do?"

"I'm gonna get married and have a family. I wasn't plannin' to go to college. I ain't the college type. Goin' to work for Dad."

Worry creased my brow as I peered at him from under shielded lids.

"Hey, it's cool; you just worry about the race. Get a load of that skuzz bucket!" he pointed over the dash.

My eyes stuck to Franky for a minute, searching for sincerity. Was he really happy about the turn his life was taking? When I saw absolutely no doubt that he was happy, my eyes followed his finger.

"Man, that is the ugliest car. Bet it's souped up, though!"

"You know it!"

"I guess I better go put in my fee and draw. Gonna be a long a night with all these cars here."

"Didja see the bean wagon over there?"

"Ha! Probably hauls ass, too. All these cars are race cars, man! From all over the county," I gazed around, awed by the number of cars racing tonight, some just starting out, trying to beat established racers, some having worked their way up at other races to try out for the champ. That's where I was now. At the end. The final race.

"Yep, quick count, fifteen races before the final," Franky patted the dash, "and there's only one big winner tonight! And she's right here!"

"Yeah," I nodded, smiled and popped open the door, "Hang loose; I'll be right back."

Kids started crowding around my car, checking out the '57. "You're lookin' at the county champ car, right here. Anybody interested in a little side action?" Franky always had a way of making me laugh. I shook my head as I walked away.

Life was moving too fast for me, but fast was the ticket tonight.

Franky and I stayed in or near the car during the first fourteen races, up by the starting line. A race as important as the one I was entered in tonight required someone to stay by the car at all times so nobody could jack with it.

When I left, Franky stayed; when he left, I stayed.

Nobody, and I mean nobody, could be allowed alone with one of the race cars. The final race yielded three thousand dollars, which meant increased opportunity for hanky-panky of a race car. I wasn't about to let anyone near my baby!

Franky pulled a smoke from his pocket.

"Not in the car, man!" I couldn't stand the smell of cigarettes. He knew that.

"I was takin' it outside. Besides, the windows are down," he shrugged.

"Yeah, but the last time you smoked in here with the windows down it took me two weeks to get rid of the smell," I rolled my eyes. For a best friend, he sure had some nasty habits. I loved him anyway. And so did Joanie.

As the fourth race lined up at the start, I thought of Joanie. She was stacked. There would never be another like her in my life, and she belonged to him. Visions of her greeting me at the door when I came home from work, pregnant stomach protruding into me as I hugged her, caused me to miss the rubber burning, smoke rolling take off. The more I thought about Joanie, the more I worried I was falling for her. I couldn't let that happen. I stared out the windshield at Franky, puffing away, trash talking the lead car until it was no longer visible.

"Did you see that? Holy smoke! That car had a takeoff, now! He ain't gonna beat out this beauty, though!" Franky's head poked through the driver's window.

"It's only the fourth race, Franky," I pointed out. "He may not even be in it after this one. And I drew number eleven, so…"

"Either way, I'm lookin' at the champ right now!"

Donna and Joanie reappeared and I flushed with guilt. "Where's the pop, Franky?" Joanie pressed her fine body into him and pecked his cheek.

"In the trunk, baby! I'll get you one."

"I missed you," she pouted at him and he kissed her perfect lips, a long, soft, wet kiss.

"I hope I find a love like that someday," Donna scared the life out of me sticking her head in my window. "Except, it would have to be somebody better than Jerkface!" she called over the open trunk.

"Aw, shut up, Red! You annoy me like a red headed step sister!"

I chuckled.

Donna peered at me with her squinting green eyes, "I wonder if your best bud knows how you feel about his girl?" She whispered.

"Donna!" I warned.

"Don't worry. My lips are sealed. Of course, if Dad is really mad because I slipped out and I get severely punished…"

"I'll take care of it. Just keep your noise to yourself."

She cocked her head at me. "Gee, if it were you instead of Jerkface, I'd be an aunt in seven months."

"What's that Red?" Franky sneaked up on her from behind, handing her a soda.

"Oh, I was just telling my thick headed, no romance brother, that he could be like you and make me an aunt by next year," she stuck out her tongue at me.

"Hey, don't rush him! He has big plans and my full support. Marriage ain't the way for some guys, Red."

"You can be my baby's aunt," Joanie comforted, her voice falling like honey in my buzzing bee ears.

"Thanks, Joanie!" Donna threw an arm around her shoulder and squeezed.

"Yah! But she can't be my baby's aunt!" Franky popped.

"Jerkface!" Donna exclaimed while Joanie

whined, "Franky!"

"Hey, you chicks shut up already. The next race is lining up!" Franky snarled. "Why don't you go down and join the fan line, or something, let me and my best man spend some quality time before he goes off to that fancy college life!"

"Shut up, Jerkface! You're so rude!" Donna fired back. "Hey, Joanie, there's Vicky! Let's go see if she knows anything about that cheerleader's… uhm… screw up!"

"We'll join the fan line when Davis races!" Joanie patted my arm, leaving it tingling before she and Donna hurried off.

"Mom would not like to hear that trashy gossip coming out of your mouth!" I called after Donna.

"Yeah, you talk like a sailor, Red. Maybe you'd have better luck getting together with one of them!"

"Screw you, Jerkface!"

I always feared my best friend and sister would realize one day that they were a perfect match and fall for each other the way they messed around. Then, one day, Joanie walked into Franky's life and never left. Sometimes, I wished she would, so maybe I would have a shot, but I still found that hard to think about, seeing as it would tear me and Franky apart. We'd been friends since Kindergarten.

When the tenth race lined up, butterflies took over my stomach and I chucked my half can of pop out the window. Every swallow had become a knot that grew and grew. This was the big one. I had to get it under control.

Franky sat on the hood, blowing smoke rings in the still night air. I shook my head.

"Hey, Franky, let's give 'er the once over again, huh?"

"Man, we checked her five hundred times!"

"You check the tires; I'll take another look under the hood." I turned the key and she vroomed to life.

"Alright, man. You're gonna waste all your gas, but if that's how you wanna roll..." he patted me on the shoulder. "Hey, that bean wagon put up a heck of fight, I guess. Heard some fans talkin' when they passed by. Lost by a bumper."

I pushed the hood up to listen, "Yeah, well maybe next year," I threw my half smile his way.

Franky kicked the tire on the right side, kicked it again, and moved on.

The sweet sound of my hard work on the magnificent motor calmed the creeping critters out of my belly. I slammed the hood, feeling better, but left her running to warm her up. About thirty minutes to line up. Franky dipped his head in and checked the gas gauge. "Little under full. Want me to top 'er off?"

"No, there's plenty." The problem with building a motor that rocked the world of racing was the gas guzzling it did. I bet it cost me a fourth of my winnings in gas alone. Well, that was probably an exaggeration. "Okay, man, calm down. I was funnin' ya. Breath. Want me to hang around?"

"Yeah, a few more minutes, man. I gotta go off in the bushes."

"Hey, no barfing, man! And don't pee on anybody!" Franky joked over his shoulder as I walked away.

"There he goes, the guy that's won every race so far! Think he'll take it?"

"That's one bitchin' ride he's got, but I don't know. I'll be down at the finish waiting to see, though."

I smiled to myself. I had become a local legend the past two summers. Tried for the title and lost it twice. This would be the night. I knew it, felt it, wanted it.

When I returned, Joanie was glued to Franky's lips, and his butt was glued to the hood, making me cringe. She glanced up when I opened the car door, "Oh, Davis! Good luck!" she bounced over to me and squeezed me tight.

"Good luck, Davis," Donna affectionately punched me in the arm.

"You don't need luck, man, but here's some anyway," Franky stuck out his hand.

"Thanks, guys. See ya at the finish!" I cast my charm their way and dodged into the car, waiting for my line up.

"You know where I'll be," Franky winked. He liked to stand at the finish line on the other car's side and stir up the fans by cheering for me. He was a card. He'd had to fun his way out of many fights doing that! I laughed at the memories. These days would soon be gone, and I would begin another life, in another land, and hopefully finish it with someone I loved.

In my rear window, the old Ford pickup serving as a fan transport stopped at Franky's whistle. The driver greeted him, teased Donna, and checked out

Joanie.

Yes, I would miss these days and remember them forever. My mind focused on the line, I didn't realize just how much I would miss them.

$B\mathcal{Y}$ my fourth race, I knew my baby and I would take it all! Franky caught the transport truck back a few times to help me out. Fortunately, nobody had wrecked. A few had hit the dirt, spun off the road, and had to forfeit, but no wrecks. Wrecks meant reschedules because of the clean up. Some wrecks meant breaking it up all together.

"I knew it, man! You had 'im by a mile!" Franky's grin filled his face.

"Yeah, yeah, but now comes the tough one. Last year's winner." The previous winner was the only one that didn't have to draw in the second round. He had the fastest car. It would be tough. I had worked on my motor until I got her the needed speed, though. This race was all gonna come down to the driving.

"You'll beat him, man!"

I smiled at Franky. I was really gonna miss him. There was no way I would ever share the secret with him, the reason I won, what kept me going. Seeing Joanie's face at the head of the fan line, cheering for me, that's what brought me across that line first. I pictured her perfect lips calling my name at the start of every race, and ran my baby as fast as she could go to get to that beautiful face on the other end. No way could I ever tell my best friend that.

"This is it, man, all the marbles!"

"Yep. The last one," I looked deep into his eyes. Our lives would never be the same after this night.

"Hey, man, when we're old and gray, we'll be tellin' our grandsons they don't know anything about racing!"

"Yeah," I guess Franky noticed the sadness in my eyes, because for the first time in our friendship, he hugged me. Hugging was not manly. "Smoke 'im, man!"

"I will," and I believed it too.

As I lined up, engine revving at the start up, I imagined Joanie waiting for me, calling out for me as always. I revved my motor again, the car next to me answering, the driver sneering at me, talkin' trash. I kept my mind on Joanie. I had to get to her before the skuzz-bucket next to me, and I would.

Four streaks of black rubber, rolls of billowing smoke and an even takeoff later, I was sure I had him, and seconds later, the unimaginable happened, changing our lives forever.

$\mathcal{I}$ had to find Joanie! She had to help me out of this mess! She was the only one who could. I couldn't get on with my life without her. I'd been everywhere looking for her, but she was nowhere to be found. And then, on the last leg of my search, the last crowded school hallway, through all of the rich, randy, rowdy heads bobbing and bouncing about, a girl caught my eye, making me momentarily forget why I was at my old school in the first place.

Though I finally remembered, my shifted search

only provided glimpses of this new girl here and there the rest of the day. By the end of the day, I was sure she was the one. If anybody was my Joanie, it was her. No girl in my life had made me forget Joanie. Not since the first night Franky and I met her at the drive in where we stopped for a burger, Franky's treat. This girl roaming the halls in search of someone, hair a mess in a loose ponytail bun, strands falling down her alabaster neck and shoulders, around her slender refined face, and that look of lost love in her sad eyes, was a goddess. My goddess.

The plain clothes adorning her body only drew attention to the figure she obviously tried to hide, though she probably didn't intend it. Those ripped jeans, and that thinning, faded, oversized sweatshirt... mmhm.

She was the hottest girl I'd seen in my life. Definitely the most beautiful, natural, angelic girl I'd ever seen. Thoughts of her pushed Joanie from my mind, an impossible feat. She had to be the one for me. This was the love I had avoided all my life. This was the love I could no longer avoid. There was no way I would be able to put this chick out of my mind! No way!

She filled every second of my thoughts after that first glimpse. I floated through the crowded, then emptied hallways, but I didn't learn a thing about her, didn't see her anywhere, couldn't figure out where she was, who she was. After winning that final race, my number one goal in life had changed and now it had been replaced with a desperate desire to meet that girl, make her mine. I could think of nothing else.

I overheard some guys in the courtyard talking about a girl, about going over to a house after school at the end of the week to take care of the yard, something about her and her mother being in a car accident. It was really noisy out there from all the construction work on the new gym at school, and I barely heard the address, but my instincts told me they were talking about her.

Was it that familiar look in her eyes, the look of loss, of death, of loneliness that attracted me? I felt the look all too well. I had lost someone very important to me the night of the race.

Maybe that's it, why I found her so uncontrollably attractive. We had something in common. I couldn't believe that I just noticed her, all the times I've been here, looking for Joanie, trying to catch her so I could talk to her.

With each thought I had about her, though, a brick stacked in my mind. My wall of defense already held a row at the foundation. Very few girls had ever caught my attention before, and when they did, I soon discovered they weren't what they claimed. I never let them spoil my long-term plans with their short-term goals. I mean, I wasn't like other guys, like Franky. No babies were spilling forth from these loins before I accomplished what I had set out to do. In my opinion, two people in a relationship were supposed to complement each other, stick by each other, and help each other achieve their goals, like my parents did until…

I didn't need any girls dragging me down with them.

Was this girl different? She seemed to be just who she was and she appeared to have her own goals. I could tell by looking at her that she was focused only on those goals, too. Could I trust her to be who she was?

My plans had changed after the race. College never came, and I became determined to find Joanie after our fight.

Maybe it wasn't really love, maybe it was just

time. Time to have a life. Maybe that's why I just noticed her.

I drifted through the rest of the day dreaming of her, wondering about her goals, wondering if there would be an us in my future. My next step: going by that house those guys were talking about to see if it was where she lived and trying to find a way to get her attention.

My problem with Joanie could wait.

This new girl had to notice me.

I needed her to notice me.

I was ready to know love.

When I saw the flowers, I knew it was the right house. So many flowers covered the porch!

I had a feeling most of those flowers came from neighbors who had never known them.

It was that way at my house when…

My thoughts screeched to a stop as a newer model car pulled up to the curb and my dream girl exited, gliding into my peripheral vision. I thought to myself, Man, they sure don't make cars like my '57 anymore!

Realizing I stood in the open, diagonal from her

house, I ducked behind a hedge, peeking through the baring branches, gobbling glimpses of her. If she saw me staring at her house, she'd think I was a perv or something. A pale yellow glow seemed to surround her in the afternoon sun. The car drove past, forcing me further behind the shrub, more out of her view, but my eyes remained on her. She was absolutely beautiful. My heart thumped; my breaths quickened.

But, how could I even talk to her?

I'd never get the nerve up to meet her. It wasn't shyness or anything like that. I didn't want to get to know her if it would only hurt her later. I had to find Joanie, fast. She was the only one who could help me, the only way I could have a relationship with this girl. I wish Joanie wasn't dodging me like this. It's not like all the blame belonged to her.

Watching this new girl turn up the sidewalk, slow steps, feet dragging, hesitant to enter as she reached the front door, I started to feel like a peeping tom. I glanced around nervously expecting a police officer to jump out at me and slap some handcuffs on.

Now that would make a great first impression!

The thought made me smile, though

embarrassment over spying on her filled my conscience.

As she reached for the doorknob, she paused and peered over her shoulder, searching the hedge.

It made me remember that feeling I used to get sometimes when I undressed before bed, that 'somebody's watching me feeling?' Obviously, she sensed me watching her. Her body followed in a slow circle while she gazed around, and immediately, I turned my back acting like I inspected the hedge, glancing from the corner of my eye. Once her circle completed, she pushed aside some flowers with her toe and entered the house. My eyes remained on her door for some time wishing she would come back out.

A breath escaped my lips, a long drawn out sigh I had held in while she searched the hedge. Man, she was so pretty!

I had it bad.

I had to meet her, but what about Joanie? Donna? What would I tell my dream girl about them?

Or worse, what would Donna tell her if they happened to meet?

The sudden obsession, the determination, the

quick thinking all fell into motion at the same time, just like when I raced that last race.

How could I meet her? I had to focus on that. The rest would follow once that happened. It had to. Love always prevailed, didn't it?

Waiting for her to come back outside wasn't the answer.

Just go up and knock on the door, offer your sympathy. Tell her about…

No! I didn't want her to like me because of that. I didn't want our relationship to begin with sympathy.

Certainly she would come back out, later, I told myself as the sun slid lower behind the houses on the street.

But, she never came back outside.

While darkness grew about me, shadows falling from objects blocking the false lighting of street lamps, I resolved to try again another day.

I spent the next three days at my old school searching for her, learning about her, hiding behind that hedge watching her come home.

Every day the same car dropped her off.

Every day she toed new flowers aside, not bothering to pick any up and take them in.

Every day I felt more like a stalker.

Was love supposed to turn you into a stalker? Surely not. The thought of my dad's large frame hiding behind a hedge, watching my mother's every move, made me laugh. Did Dad spend hours watching Mom before the meeting he told me about several times? Was that spontaneous encounter actually planned out by dear old Dad? Tears pooled as I thought about Mom and Dad, their love for each other, the love I always wanted. I missed them so much.

Every daydream girl carried that same sad look on her face. Did she miss her mother like I missed mine? Seeing her unhappiness increased my desire to make her smile, make her feel special, make her feel loved.

In the entire time I'd spent watching her, nobody ever showed up to visit.

Nobody stopped to ask if she needed anything. I recalled our house stayed full of people, friends, family, for months after the accident.

The guys that had talked earlier in the week about taking care of her lawn pushed mowers and carried weeders down the street, startling me to action.

Spontaneous meeting coming up, I imagined myself saying to Dad. In my mind a deep, proud chuckle flowed from his belly to his mouth as he patted me on the back, "Go get 'er, son!"

I joined the mower squad to see if I could help. Maybe when she heard all the noise, she would come outside and I could introduce myself. Perfect plan!

"Hey, guys!" I waved a hand in the air, falling in behind them. "I heard you at lunch the other day. Need some help?"

"Well, it's not a very big yard. It won't take long." The one swinging the weeder shrugged.

I swung in beside them and crossed the street to her house.

But, it might be just long enough!

As the guys readied their mowers and weeders in the front yard, I moved around to the side of the house where a set of hedge clippers laid waiting. I bent to pick up the hedge clippers so I could trim the scruffy limbs when my eyes grazed the window to my right, no blinds, no curtains, just a clear view of a messy bun of beautiful brunette hair.

The clippers lay just out of reach on the ground below my left hand, but seeing her made me straighten for a better look. I peeked through the corner of the window, trying to keep out of her view.

She was lying face down on a bed, her head buried into a pillow up to her delicately shaped ears.

Sleeping? "She wouldn't be sleeping on her face, dork," I mumbled to myself.

She was crying. I could see it now, the jerky movements of her shoulders as they rose and fell with each sob.

Quelling the urge to run into her house and hold her, I thought of my own tears falling, seemingly not so long ago.

After a few moments, the noise of the lawn mowers crept through the sealed doors and windows, and roared to life in her ears. I saw her head rise from the pillow and I ducked. When I chanced a peek through the bare glass again, she sat with her back to me, wiping her eyes with the palms of her hands. She smashed the pillow she now held into her face and inhaled deeply.

I recognized that action. I knew exactly what she was doing, trying to remember the scent of her mother.

I looked away again. I don't know how many times I did that after…

When I turned back, she was gone.

I never heard the front door creak.

MEL

$\mathcal{I}$ couldn't believe it!

I'd fallen out on Mom's bed after my long day at school. At first I was daydreaming, which I rarely do, but I couldn't stop thinking about that guy.

Where had he come from? Would I see him again? I'd caught sight of him a few more times this past week, roaming the halls with that searching look on his face. Was he searching for me? Questions about him ricocheted through my head. I never seemed to get close enough for him to notice me.

Was I just obsessed with him because of my loneliness, because I had nobody else? Schoolwork and graduating had faded from my mind since the accident. How would that fading affect my future plans? What was I going to do now?

Then, as much as I hated to admit it, I fell into a 'Why me?' episode. If anyone had known Mom and me, they wouldn't understand that. Kath would have slapped me silly if she were in the room with me. I didn't understand it. I mean, we pretty much hated each other, me and mom. At least that's what I always thought, felt. So, why all of these tears for her? In a twinkle of time, I went from a sense of euphoria over Mr. Hottie, to depression over having no mother to share this amazing news with, no money with which to make myself over, and no idea what would happen to me in the immediate future; my emotions tumbled like an out of balance washing machine.

My face stuffed into Mom's pillow, I started to

meditate, or, pray, or whatever you're supposed to do when you're sad and alone. And just when I started talking to that Higher Power...the Ultimate Being of the Universe... or, God...

SOME INCONSIDERATE JERK STARTED MOWING HIS LAWN!

I pushed up, wiped my weepy eyes with my palms, sniffled, and mashed my face into Mom's pillow, again. Just one more smell... just enough to remember…

The pillow dropped from my lap when I straightened.

Remember what? Why did I want to remember her scent? All I had to do was go dig that vodka bottle out of the trashcan, open it, and take a big whiff. My face burned with embarrassment and anger. I was so angry with her for leaving me alone!

Surely we'd had some good times.

I just couldn't remember any of them.

It didn't matter now, because right now, all my rage and pain redirected itself onto that ridiculous idiot who had nerve enough to mow the lawn during my time of sorrow!

And then, as I stomped out of the room toward

the front door, a reflection in the dresser mirror caught my eye! My rush of anger moved me on to the front door, even though my instincts instructed me that the reflection was him— Mr. Hottie! My depressed and tormented mind played tricks on me! Surely my dream guy was not some peeping perv!

"Grrrrrr!" I growled as I flung the door open to five or six guys from school, mowing my lawn, weeding around my house, and raking chopped up grass and leaves into little piles.

Instant tears of caring and gratitude rolled down my cheeks.

I was supposed to YELL! SCREAM! SMACK SOME NEIGHBOR!

But, there they were... in my yard.

Sure, now I get their attention.

I rolled my eyes, slammed the door, sat on the floor, and cried into my folded arms.

I couldn't even have a pity party alone.

My head popped up when I remembered the reflection! Was he one of the guys out there? He wasn't in the group on the front lawn, but I had seen him at the side of the house.

In one swift move I rose from the floor,

stumbled back to Mom's room, and breathed myself into control before I entered. Like a spy, I pressed my body against the wall behind the doorframe and slightly bent my head forward to glimpse the window reflected in the mirror.

My shoulders slumped.

He wasn't there anymore.

It must have been my imagination.

I had been thinking about him, and then crying over Mom and my situation. Obviously, it had all just blended into a hallucination.

Turning to the bathroom to wash my tear stained face, I readied for the mall trip the girls and I planned at lunch. One look at my swollen, red-rimmed eyes in the mirror held me hostage there until the noise outside halted, after which I slipped to my room to change, pulling the blinds and curtains closed first on the chance that I wasn't imagining him.

Maybe I was too modest and should be more forward like Ruthie or Mags, leaving the blinds up, but I couldn't bring myself to do that. After all, I lived alone now.

DAVIS

As I neared the front corner of the house, the door slammed shut.

I missed her. She hadn't even stepped outside, though. Boldly moving to the porch and raising my hand to knock, I suddenly froze. My intention had been to apologize for our noise, but just like a game of freeze tag from my youth, some imaginary friend, probably Franky, yelled, "Freeze!"

Another row of bricks extended the height of my wall.

No matter how I tried, I just couldn't bring my hand to the doorframe, my fear a magnetic polar to the wood only inches away.

What if she yelled at me?

What if I saw hurt and rejection in her gorgeously searching dark eyes?

My head dropped.

My hand fell to my side.

Damn it! I knew she was in there crying, and my cowardice wouldn't allow me to interrupt, to offer words of condolence, to comfort, but my imaginary self, the one that hugged long forgotten pregnant Joanie after a hard day at work, held my dream girl and dried her tears with my shoulder.

The real world timing just wasn't right.

The action wasn't appropriate, not now.

I couldn't offer her sympathy, though it would be sincere, just to get to know her.

Waiting seemed the only answer, so I stepped off the porch as the mowing equipment died off, one by one. The guys gathered the tools they brought, gas cans, hedge clippers, weeders, and met at the curb.

Reluctantly, I fell into step behind them, but with one final glance over my shoulder, maybe a grateful wave.

Nope. She was nowhere to be seen.

Somebody else was making herself visible, though. As I turned back to follow the guys, Donna stood behind my peeping hedge.

How long had she been there? Had she seen me at the door? The imaginary voice in the freeze tag game suddenly became not so imaginary.

My eyes drew near closed in anger while heat rose to my face.

She had no right to spy on me!

She had no right to stop me from living! Not now!

College was in the past and she should be, too.

Her green eyes flashed at me as I neared her, following closely behind the guys.

I wanted to slap the smug off of her face, but I just kept moving as if she wasn't there.

MEL

Frantically, I pulled clothes from my drawers, my closet, the laundry hamper, searching for something, anything sexy, presentable! As I changed, I realized I'd been wearing the same type of outfit all week! I had to throw out these baggy, worn sweatshirts and faded tee shirts.

They were only good for my running. Locating

my only black bra, black cami, and second hand fitted yellow tee, and my best jeans— which were in the hamper— I pulled a ninety-second change.

I slipped back into Mom's room to peek out the window.

It had been him!

The group of guys from my yard pushed mowers and carried other equipment while they slumped down the street, and tagging along behind them was my mystery guy! Hands stuck in the front pockets of his Levis, hair fluttering in the breeze, and saunter drawing my eyes to his back pockets. I watched him until a moan of desire slipped from my throat and I bit my lower lip. I had never been this attracted to a guy before.

Never!

What was wrong with me all of a sudden? Where was my focus?

When he glanced back over his shoulder, I ducked out of the window so he wouldn't see me peeping at him. I wanted to wave, to say thanks to the mower squad, but mainly to acknowledge him, make him notice me; I just couldn't. I forced myself past my shyness to try. Slipping closer to the window, my hand in midair, I held my breath and searched the street, but they had already moved too far away to see me.

Why did I dodge behind the window frame when he turned around? I chastised myself with the question.

I was so confused.

I guess it was good that I hid because I didn't want to meet him and discover that he just felt sorry for me, anyway. I wanted him to like me, not feel sorry for me and with his reflection still fresh in my mind, my forehead thumped the window, a sharp breath escaping my lips.

When would be a good time to meet him?

Would I ever?

My body fell limply backward onto the fluffy bed while my mind fell into a vivid daydream of how this afternoon could have gone:

Knock, knock on my door, "I'm sorry for intruding, us making all of this noise, at such a horrible time. It's really sad about your mother. Is there anything I can do for you? I mean, bedsides mow the yard?" His deep, quiet voice flowed through the screen, instant comfort.

"Please, come in," I directed, cheeks still wet with tears.

Seeing my damp face, red-rimmed eyes, and downturned mouth, he rushed to me as my sobs became uncontrollable and he wrapped his tight arms around me, causing my head to fall to his strong shoulder. "It'll be okay," he whispered into my hair. "You're not alone anymore. It'll be okay. You'll be okay," and then, as I lifted my face to his, he would kiss me tenderly.

In my dreams, he remained until I fell asleep, holding me, stroking my hair, cuddling me with a promise to return the next night.

Hugging myself, as he might, the dream carried me away into a deep, vision filled sleep. When I awoke to the blare of a car horn, dark peered at me through the window. I glanced at the bedside clock, disbelieving I had slept for nearly two hours.

My stomach grumbled at me.

I'd missed dinner again.

Rocky Road ice cream called to me from the freezer, but I promptly responded to the car horn, grabbed my jacket and slammed the front door on my way out, knowing we would grab something to eat at the mall.

DAVIS

$\mathcal{I}$ slouched in the overstuffed chair aimed at the television set. Some dumb show about ghosts filled the screen, but images of her filled my mind.

I didn't even know her name, yet. In the hollows and caves where sleeping thoughts lie, I held her closely, warm tears pooling and spreading on my T-shirted shoulder. My hands tingled with possible connections to her soft skin. My lips met her forehead, her cheeks, and her upturned mouth. My hand drifted to her hair tie and pulled gently, allowing her silky hair to fall over my arms, delicately drifting cobwebs of delight.

Before my dream could carry me away, a loud rumble traveled up from the pit of my stomach to the drums of my ears. Rocky Road ice cream called to me from the freezer, and I promptly responded. When I opened the freezer, though, there wasn't any ice cream.

A trip down memory lane, a sudden urge to visit the mall, led me to fulfill my craving.

The mall wasn't far from Franky's old house. About a mile run and I would be there. It was a nice night for a run. I loved to run. Besides, then I would earn the ice cream, too.

The mall crawled with teenagers, as always on a Friday night. I slipped through them easily to the escalator in the center of the hall. The food court, located in the middle of the mall, resided on both the first and second floors, but the ice cream shop was upstairs. All I wanted was ice cream. A shrill wolf whistle cut through the crowd from above and for a split second all heads turned and silence filled my ears. Funny how a wanton whistle could still silence a crowd of teenagers! I shook my head in amazement as my feet touched the bottom step and I glided to the top.

Finding an empty chair in the food court at this time on a Friday night deemed itself an impossible task. I retrieved my ice cream, leaned over the second story railing, and watched the people pass by below. Kids of all ages cruised the mall at this time of night, meeting each other for the first time, or for dates, or just for fun. I loved to watch the crowd.

My elbows planted on the cool faux marble surface of the rail. Chocolate, marshmallows and nuts dropped onto my tongue from the roof of my mouth as I dug my spoon into the cheap plastic double dip bowl, chewing absently while picturing her and what might have happened if I had knocked on her door this afternoon.

Chew, dream, dig, chew, dream, dig... I fell into that pattern until the plastic bowl jarred me from my alternate life by allowing my spoon to scrape its empty bottom. I drove the spoon around the edges of the dish to collect the last two or three spoonfuls, and then I stared into its chocolaty swirled bottom, not believing that my last glance at it showed it half full.

I didn't even remember eating the second half.

Well, my stomach no longer grumbled, but my mind still reeled to the point that it abruptly made my lazy butt find a trash can, drop the empty ice cream dish into its overstuffed contents, spoon rattling, and wander back to the railing. I don't know why I stayed. I only came for ice cream, or so I thought. I suppose deep down that I hoped she would come here. She was still in high school and this was the Friday night hangout. If I didn't see her here, then what?

I had to go to her.

I was supposed to go to her. I knew at that very moment that I saw her in the school that we were meant to be together.

She was the one I had been hoping would enter my life since... forever!

I turned back toward the food court, thinking I might walk the mall, formulate a plan to meet her, when there she sat!

She wasn't alone. There were three other girls with her, but it was definitely her and she dazzled amongst them without doing or saying a thing.

MEL

After the first bite, when that soft fluffy, chocolaty marshmallow touched my tongue, I vowed to live on Rocky Road ice cream for the rest of my days. If it were my last day on earth, I would stock up on Rocky Road ice cream and have it for every meal!

I also swore to myself that I would set out to

find Mr. Right, somehow. A picture of myself carrying a carton of Rocky Road wandering the earth searching for my Greek god made me chuckle.

I had to find him, find out who he was.

I promised I would skip class, Monday, run him down in the hallway and introduce myself. I had never skipped class a day in my life!

Funny how Rocky Road gave me the courage that alcohol had given my mother. Well, that and desire, I suppose. What a dangerous combination!

For a moment I slipped off into thoughts of Mother coming home, talking about some guy she met at work, complaining that she was too fat, or too old, or too ugly to catch a guy like that. Her negative slurs filled the house, "You're just like me. You'll never get a good-looking guy like this guy, either. We're just two ugly ducklings!" Then after a few shots of vodka, she'd head off to the bar to catch a good-looking guy. She never did succeed.

Her hurtful words didn't matter. I knew I wasn't ugly. I didn't have a lot of confidence in myself, but I had enough to know that I was attractive, sort of. And, thanks to my best friends, I had found a new outfit, though I chickened out on my hair and just got a trim.

With a mouthful of chocolate, marshmallow and almond heaven, I listened absently to my friends' ravings about clothes they bought, or make up, or TV shows.

When they started in on that dumb ghost show we liked to watch, I tuned in again and spooned more ice cream to my lips. My mind drifted from the girls, the ghosts, back to him and off to dreamland again, complete with him sitting beside me on my couch, two spoons feeding each other ice cream, and laughing at the stupidity of the ghost show. The ice cream cradled in my hand so his free arm could rest around my shoulder.

After wiping away escape chocolate below his lip, he kissed me, softly and then…

"Okay. Obviously we're not all present tonight! What's up?" Mags's voice broke through my fantasy.

"Well, I just can't get that new guy out of my mind! Sorry," I bit my lower lip. My friends had been so good to me and I couldn't even allow them the attention they deserved tonight.

"I'm sorry. I just can't get over…" Kathy's words became lost in the sea of voices as I glanced up at her, past her, and into the most heavenly, calm sea I had ever witnessed.

He was here, at the mall, looking at me.

I scanned his face, his messy brown hair, his flushed cheeks, taking in every second that he stood next to the rail staring in my direction.

"Oh, for Pete's sake! Is nobody listening tonight? What was the purpose of hanging out tonight if we aren't all having fun?" Ruthie slapped her hands on the table, startling Kathy and me, and then she let out a wolf whistle that nearly pierced my eardrums, drawing my attention away from him.

"Take a look at that one! Hello, baby! Where have you been all of my life? Come to mama!"

She had no shame.

My eyes glanced back toward Kathy, who was now red faced, but over her shoulder, he was gone.

Standing, I turned a complete circle searching, but nothing. I made my way to the trashcan and threw away my plastic dish, noting another with the same color of chocolate right on the top.

"Finally, somebody's getting into the night!" Mags declared behind me.

I must really need a makeover to catch his

attention. He had vanished completely after looking at me. Maybe he wasn't the one, but I sure wanted him to be.

We roamed the mall, for a while longer, window shopping, Ruthie drawing attention to us, but when we left, I didn't really feel like sleeping over at Mags'. That was always the plan after mall trips, so Ruthie and Kathy went. I was really exhausted and sure they would understand, given the loss of my mother and all.

After Kathy drove away, I took my new clothes in, and went straight to Mom's room. Her old makeup sat on her vanity table. Our skin tone was the same, so maybe I could use this makeup.

I experimented alone, but everything I did seemed too bold. Maybe just a bit of eyeliner, a little mascara? I really didn't want to change myself all that much. If he didn't like me the way I was, then he wouldn't like me. It was possible that he didn't like me anyway. He could have been staring at Mags; most guys did.

No, his probing blue eyes were definitely on you, I told myself. Of course, being socially challenged the way I was it didn't assure me much. I often misread the actions of others.

I let my hair down, brushed it to one side and then the other. His incredible eyes filled my mind. I tried to figure out what it was about him that attracted me so much. Whatever it was, I found it in those eyes. His other features were unbelievable, too, but I was an eye girl. Well, apparently I was a butt girl, also, I reasoned while thinking about him walking down the street earlier.

Was he sad? Was that it?

Maybe a bit. Maybe he had lost someone recently, too. How romantic, two lost souls finding each other through death...

My mind drifted as I brushed my hair.

The ringing of the phone startled me to reality. I didn't want to answer it. I let the machine get it, but I listened as the caller left a message. It was Lester, I mean, Grandpa.

"This is Lester. I took care of the rent and utility bills for you. Call me if you need anything. I'm sorry I haven't been... oh, never mind! I hate these damn machines!" The gruff, distant voice, the slamming down of the receiver, the lonely beep of the answering machine cutting off gave a brief moment of clarity into my mother's sad childhood. Well, he wasn't going to fill any voids for me. I didn't even know the man, really, but it was nice of him and Paula to take care of the bills.

I rose from the chair and walked over to delete the message. That's when I realized how many calls there were on the machine. I tried to remember if I had checked it at all since I came home from the hospital.

Pushing play, I sat on the edge of Mom's bed and listened to them all, pulling the brush through my hair and deleting one message after the other. Then I stopped deleting. Mom had called the night before the accident, some excuse about not making it home. I listened to it over and over, taking in her voice, her slurred words, her apology.

How many times had I heard these same words?

What struck me was the cold indifference with which Mom's message resembled her father's. A moment of comprehension, a tiny ripple in my thoughts, brought new sadness to my heart.

The last message made me jump off the bed, brush flying through the air, and feet instantly pacing.

Back and forth, push the button, repeat the message, pace.

It was my dad!

"Uhm... it's me, baby. Look, I'm sorry. I want to be there for you, but I'm kinda stuck here for now, soberin' up. I'd like to, you know, get together when I get out, maybe. I'll call again. I gotta hang up."

I hadn't heard from my dad in years!

I didn't care to either and just because Mom was out of the picture didn't mean he could just contact me and all would be honky dory between us.

I hated him and his drug addled rejections!

I never wanted to see him again! The few times I had seen him since he left, one of us wound up hurt. Our relationship should be no relationship for the sake of the parties involved.

I was eighteen and I didn't have to answer to him or see him. I figured he was in jail, or rehab, again, where he belonged. They could just keep him there for all I cared!

Anger flowed down to my index finger, punching the delete button. No need to save that one, either. There were happier thoughts in my head to ponder on, so I headed for the freezer, the small dish of ice cream at the mall having diminished long ago.

I could eat an entire carton of Rocky Road ice cream in this one sitting, but I wouldn't tonight. I just wanted a little more. I pulled the carton out, grabbed a spoon and napkin, and headed for the couch. After bringing the TV to life, I pressed the channel selector and found that ghost show the girls and I watched, which brought my mind back to Ruthie's wolf whistle, and those baby blues.

Absently, I dipped my spoon into the cold sweetness while I fantasized about him, ghosts long forgotten.

The end credits rolled and the theme song brought me back to reality. I turned off the TV. Dragging an ice cream filled belly into the kitchen, I replaced the carton lid and stuffed the ice cream into the freezer.

If this were my last day on earth, what would I do about him?

Ever since the accident, since I've tried to put a positive spin on life, I've been asking myself that question.

I would keep that question in mind when I returned to school Monday. I would seek him out if this were my last day, so why not?

Thoughts of my mystery guy were driving me nutty. I had to get out, walk, run, or do something.

Maybe the sugar rush from that ice cream wasn't helping, either. Pent up anger, energy from being home, listening to those awful messages, began to ooze from my body.

Running always helped. I pulled on my running shoes, grabbed a light jacket, and jogged to the front door, the realization that I could jog in the house at this hour of the night without somebody's slurred yelling slowing me down brought a smile to my lips. There were many things I couldn't do living under this roof when Mother was home. Now I could do them all. I could have a huge party here if I wanted, if I were that kind of person.

I wasn't the party type, though. I had only been to one party in my high school career, and that was enough. Memories of bodies dancing, much too closely, peers drinking way too much, and pairs of bodies not caring who saw them wrapped in uncontrolled desire made me cringe.

Nope, even if I wanted to, I couldn't picture that happening here.

Eager for my run, my hand touched the doorknob and my fingers tingled.

Was it fear?

Deeper darkness crept into the house from outside, but I had never feared the dark before.

It was really late. We hadn't left the mall until it closed. I glanced at the clock above the TV. Eleven on the dot.

Bah!

I waved it off, that unnerving feeling that something bad would happen if I left the house. It probably wasn't even fear, and if it was, it was due to the accident.

What would I do if... the question repeated.

I'll just jog around the block, release a little of this energy. I wouldn't be able to sleep otherwise, and besides, it's what I wanted to do.

The door swung inward and I froze.

DAVIS

When she saw me at the mall, when she searched my face, her honest beauty sizing me up, I couldn't do it.

I hadn't known she would be there, but I guess I secretly hoped she would.

I told myself twice while desire played in her eyes, to go over and introduce myself, but I just couldn't. One look into those deep chocolate eyes scared me out of it. I couldn't do that to her. If I did meet her, I wouldn't be able to tell her everything. She would flee like a frightened deer if I did.

I had to take care of the problem with Joanie first.

That's what I told myself on the way home, anyway.

In reality, I thought about those eyes filling my own, and knew it was a mistake not to try. I watched her from afar at the mall, waited and hoped for another opportunity. A few times, I could have made it happen, bumped into her while purposely exiting the store where I hid, but my brick wall tripped me up.

I left the mall at closing time, my feet taking me through darkened streets aimlessly while I dreamed of her.

Before I knew it, I was on her street working my way to her address.

I almost changed my mind on the way there, turned around, walked the opposite direction.

It was really late, but the wanton feel of her face in my hands, the touch of her soft skin, and the imaginary taste of her ice cream coated lips kept me on track. Track days, football, and tennis had made the long run from the mall easy for me. I lifted my arm, sniffed, and wiped away streaks of sweat at my temples. A few deep breaths calmed my racing heart.

I stood in the street, before the curb where the car had dropped her off several times during the week, staring at her small, white house growing larger as I moved up the walk.

What did I think I was doing?

Old lessons from my parents crept into my thoughts as I turned back down the walk toward the street, pacing: "Never visit a friend after nine at night," Mother warned in my mind. "Unless you want to get shot," Dad chimed in.

So there I was, pacing up to the steps, then back again, about to get shot.

"How are you going to explain your late visit, dufus?" I asked myself.

She probably wasn't even home yet, anyway. People had made it a habit to leave lights on when they weren't home, deterring unwanted visitors from taking everything they owned while they were away. Light filtered only through the front window blinds, so it was possible she was still out.

The thought lifted my courage, forcing me onward.

Lost in schemes of what to say if she was home, plans rolling through my mind, I absently paced up the two steps to the door just before it swung inward, leaving only a screen between us.

I froze, speechless.

18

MEL

The porch light reflected the tiny beads of sweat on his forehead.

His chest rose and fell with slightly winded breaths.

His surprised eyes twinkled as they wandered over my face, hair, lips.

I wanted to speak, but words lost out as my eyes searched his face, my breathing matching his, and my shyness suddenly overcame me, forcing me to drop my eyes to the hole at the bottom of the screen door.

"Hi!" His greeting touched my ears like the wings of a thousand butterflies, softly, full of wonder and undeclared love. My eyes moved up to meet his smiling ones.

"Hi!" The corners of my mouth turned up in response.

I couldn't believe he was standing on my porch!

"Uhm...I was here earlier, with some guys from the school... mowing," he stammered.

"I know. Thank you!" Thank you? Really! Can you be more original?

DAVIS

What was I doing here?

I couldn't even talk to her without making a fool of myself. Her beauty left me speechless. Besides, the relationship wouldn't go far, ruined before it started, another brick clinked onto my wall.

I had to get away from her, but neither my eyes nor my feet would budge.

"So... uh... if you need anything else... I mean... uh..."

Wow! Could I sound more pathetic?

MEL

Oh, my gosh! We already had something in common! He was shy, too. It was so cute to see him stammer for something to say. It relaxed me, made me glad it wasn't me doing the talking. My voice raced to rescuc him from himself. "Uhm, actually, I had this sudden burst of energy and I was thinking of going for a walk or something, you know? But, it's kind of late, and dark, and well, would you like, come with me?"

Oh, my gosh! You did not seriously just make yourself sound afraid. You are not afraid of anything!

His features relaxed, "Sure!" he nodded. "Uhm, my name's Davis."

My body temperature rose just being this near to him! Flames licked the screen door while he stood there, looking in. Despite the chill in the night air, the fire spread through my body beginning at my flushed face and creeping slowly downward. When it reached my knees, they almost buckled under.

I couldn't believe he just showed up, this late.

It seemed impossible that this was happening, the line between fantasy and reality crumbling at my doorstep.

I unlocked the screen door, and he held it open, "Mel... uh, Amelia," I corrected as I looked up into his gorgeous face, a faint smile playing on my lips. Our eyes met, held, and then quickly looked down the porch steps. Weakly, my feet stumbled on the first one and his hand gripped my elbow for support. I swore to myself that if I checked my elbow when I got home it would have third degree burns in the shapes of his fingertips!

Letting the screen door slam shut, he followed me down the steps and soon walked in sync at my side.

"Amelia? That's a pretty name," he glanced down at me.

"My friends call me Mel. I prefer Mel. It's okay if you call me Mel." Shut up! You're blabbering! My inner self screamed.

DAVIS

She was definitely the one. I knew it as soon as she spoke, and then touching her, and her blabbering about her name, confirmed it. She was more beautiful up close than she was from a distance. Her voice fluttered into my ears, the sweet sound of dripping nectar to a hummingbird. I finally found her; she made my heart race.

My hand drifted closer to hers as we glided down the dimly lit street. What would she do if I reached out for it? Cautiously, I fell into step with her, allowing my hand to swing closer, barely brushing hers. A light tremor began at my knuckles, spreading hopefully up my arm and straight to my racing heart. Wondering if she felt it too, I glanced down just as she met my gaze, the desire in her eyes matching mine. She had felt it.

MEL

Whoa! The most incredible sensation in the world just left me wanting more. I longed for him to reach out and take my hand in his! The silence overwhelmed me. "So, where are you from?" I prodded.

DAVIS

Whew! That was a tough first question. Would she believe me if I answered her honestly? Probably not, "I stay a few blocks away. Well, more

MEL

My brows drew together in warning when his voice caught and he answered so vaguely. It sounded as if he didn't want to tell me. Or, maybe he couldn't tell me. Curious, I thought. But, he seemed like a nice guy. And the electricity between us couldn't be denied. When he touched my hand, I thought I would die from the charge running through me. Does it matter where he's from if he's the one and you know it? Maybe he has secret he's hiding, a parent like my mother. I used to hide her all of the time, too.

"Across town? Really? And you just happened to be in the neighborhood?"

"Well, yes, no, I run a lot and this just happened to be the place I wound up."

"Huh, me, too! I mean, I run. I love running.

So, not knocking you running, but that's an awful long way. Why didn't you just drive?"

DAVIS

"Uhm, I, uh, didn't want to," I couldn't tell her the truth about my '57. Not yet.

"Speaking of the mall, I saw you there earlier."

"Yeah, I saw you, too."

"Why'd you run off? Why didn't you say hello or something?" she looked up at me and I had to turn away, collect my thoughts. Why did I run off?

"I didn't. I mean, my sister was bugging me and all. Besides, you have some pretty forward friends, there. That red head comes on strong. Maybe she kind of scared me off."

"Oh, yeah," she laughed, "that's Ruthie. She is pretty forward, but she's fun to hang out with. So you have a sister? I never had the problem of being bugged by a brother or sister, luckily. Mags, the girl with the green streaks in her hair? She's one of seven. She's right in the middle. Three are adults and moved away. It's a trip staying at her house with all those younger kids running around. Her parents are great!"

"Hmph! I bet. You are lucky, not having anyone to pester you."

MEL

Blocks of houses passed us and the night so quiet, still, exaggerated the silent moments between us, our footsteps barely breaking the sound barrier. Swing chains squeaked, the noise carrying eerily in the slight breeze, drawing my attention. I hadn't sat on a swing since I was in elementary school. I couldn't resist the feeling of freedom it brought to my overwhelmed heart; that dubious lift of tense desire led me up the curb onto the spongy grass slope toward the dangling rubber seats in the park.

* * *

DAVIS

At first, shock filled me as she started toward the swings, but I quickly realized she didn't know about the last time I was here, at this very park, my '57 pulled to the curb awaiting my best friend, motor revving. My nineteen-year-old emotions still raged at my sister's face popping up over the seat.

Pushing the negative thoughts from my mind, watching her take to the swing like a bird in flight, caused me to lose a few years, my heart feeling younger, too. I parked it next to her, turning so I could see her face in the moonlight. Her delicate, unpolished fingers wrapped around the chains, she floated back and forth, a smile of past innocence playing on her lips. Twice I stopped myself from pulling her off the swing and wrapping her in my arms. The camera in my mind filmed our kiss, one of her sneaker clad feet popping up behind her.

Sheeesh! I really needed to stop watching corny movies. I chuckled to myself.

"What's so funny?" Her question trailed from behind me to in front of me, her face turned toward me, brows furrowed, lips downturned.

"I was just thinking about something." Heat of embarrassment rose to my face.

MEL

His face darkened in the moonlight, the pink barely visible in the pale light surrounding the small park.

What was he thinking about?

I dragged my feet to slow my pendulum body to a stop. "Well, I'm always up for a laugh," I prodded.

"Nah, it's really not that funny. It was just a thought," he turned away, eyes searching the ground.

"Oh," the realization that he might have been laughing at me, swinging like a child, rushed out in a breath.

I stood, ready to leave him there alone.

"No! I wasn't laughing at you! I was thinking about something and..." He jumped from the swing as I stepped away.

"Well, if you weren't laughing at me, then why can't you tell me what you were thinking about?"

I knew it was too good to be true. He was just too good looking to like me. Somebody must have put him up to this... paid him on a bet! It wouldn't be the first time that had happened to me! I recalled a time in middle school that a high school guy bet another that he wouldn't ask me out. It infuriated me! That was the day I decided love could wait.

And how cruel for him to do that now! This was not the time for sick jokes. Heat of anger rose to my face.

DAVIS

Great! Now she's mad! What am I going to do? Before she stormed away, I reached for her arm.

It was now or never. No turning back after this.

MEL

In mid step I felt his fingers curl around my elbow the way they had when he supported me in my trip down the porch, and in a breath of time, his arms embraced me.

"I wasn't laughing at you; I was smiling because I was thinking about this." His quiet words brushed my face just before his gentle lips pressed against mine. Another current of warmth spread from my welcoming mouth to my face, and then down my neck and onward. A lump formed in my throat; it must have been my heart; it had beat so fast it was ready to jump right out of place, escaping to follow him wherever he went. Anger forgotten, sick jokes chased from my mind by his tenderness, my lips responded.

* * *

DAVIS

As I lifted my head, I waited for the slap that never came.

Her eyes remained closed; her flushed face tilted upward toward mine, her breathing shallow.

MEL

I was dreaming. I knew I was dreaming. I must have fallen asleep on that lumpy old couch at home, the carton of Rocky Road melting on the floor where I dropped it. If I opened my eyes, I would find out that this wasn't real. He had not stopped by the house; we had not walked to the park; he had not just kissed me. I had only dreamed it.

If I opened my eyes, the wonderful warm

feeling of his embrace would leave me with the chill of the night. I'd had dreams like this before, mainly about movie stars, when I was young and alone. I didn't want to open my eyes because I knew he would be gone.

The warmth at my waist not dissipating with the chill, I had to open my eyes.

DAVIS

Her lids lifted slowly, as if from sleep, and I could see the uncertainty in the rich coffee and lime colors that twinkled beneath the moon.

Then, she smiled; she didn't slap me; her lips curled at the corners in a simply sweet smile of approval.

My heart thumped with the realization of love and swiftly melted into her hands. We belonged together, just like Franky and Joanie had belonged together.

* * *

MEL

Forcing my eyes open, his perfect blue clad chest focused into view, then his faultless neck, incredibly chiseled chin, jawbone and slightly flushed cheeks tightened with caution. Cobalt eyes tensed momentarily, and then sparkled in response to my smile. For the first time in my life, I was in love.

MEL

$\mathcal{My}$ fingers curled into his; our moist nervous palms pressed together as our steps blended. I leaned my head into his shoulder. "So, why have I never noticed you around school before?"

"Maybe because I already graduated. I've spent the last week there trying to find somebody. I just wasn't expecting that somebody to be you, but I'm glad it was," one side of his lip rose in a half grin as I gazed up at him; his smile melted my heart again.

DAVIS

We strolled around the block, talking, laughing, getting to know one another. I had waited a lifetime, and then some, for the girl to come around, and she squeezed my hand at that very moment. Her soft chocolate hair doused in strawberry scents drove me insane. When her eyes crinkled up at me in question, or smile, the urge to embrace her overwhelmed my senses. I had never felt this way before. Even feelings of Joanie, as I dreamt she was mine, were never this strong.

I had waited and waited for this since the race, and now she was here. I couldn't wait to tell Franky…

And I would have to let her go. How could I let her go? I just knew that when she discovered the truth, she would leave me.

The thought ripped at my heart, creating a pain

so intense, my eyes glistened and I winced.

MEL

"What's wrong?" I never believed in love at first sight, even though I had read about it in those mushy romance novels. When he winced, the slightest squeeze of my hand, I cringed as a stab of shock shot up my arm, my empathy for him so strong already.

DAVIS

"Nothing, I was thinking about someone lost to me." I wasn't totally evading the truth.

MEL

* * *

"I'm sorry, I lost my mother recently." I hadn't felt a pain that strong, though. He must have really loved that person he was thinking about. Was it a girl? Had they broke up? Was that who he had been looking for at the school?

Mentioning my mother made me recall a slurred statement she graciously threw out at me whenever I shared exciting news with her, "If iths too good to be thrue, then it iths."

Was this too good to be true? It was happening so fast.

Was I rebounding emotionally from the loss of my mother?

Had the accident awakened a desperate desire that could no longer wait?

Was he still in love with the one he had lost?

I glanced up at the look of concern hovering in his lowered eyes, long dark lashes shielding them from the moon's gentle rays.

So what if the accident had stirred this feeling? So what if he had lost someone and longed for them? The feelings we shared now were real, and they weren't one sided. Whoever it was, she would remain lost to him as our love grew!

Happiness flooded me, more than I'd known in my life, and I intended to hold on to it as long as possible. And whoever it was that hurt him now, hurt me through him, and we could deal with the pain together, couldn't we?

I wanted to help him, be with him.

Hand in hand, we strolled up the sidewalk to her porch where this wonderfully weird night started.

DAVIS

"So, I'll see you in the halls?" Her brows arched playfully.

"What's wrong with tomorrow?" I leaned toward her angelic face just as she tilted her chin up.

"Nothing," she whispered into my lips.

"Maybe we could go running in the morning, start the day off getting sweaty..." Did I just say that? It sounded more like Franky's line.

"Great," I felt the brush of her lips on mine as

she faintly spoke the word.

And then, my lips pressed against hers, my tongue searching for the dark cavern of her mouth, and finally meeting her warm, moist, softness in a long good night kiss, the only parts of our bodies touching.

MEL

The warmth returned when his soft lips met mine. I didn't want the night to end, but at least we had found each other, knew each other, now. And we were going to spend time together tomorrow, if not just the morning, doing my favorite of all things, running.

I floated through the doorway, stopping at the phone to call the girls, but the time read two in the morning. Had we walked that long? Instead, I waltzed to my bedroom where I lay awake without light for the rest of the darkest part of the morning, reliving the night.

The smile on my face followed me into my

dreams just as dawn crackled through the slits in my blinds.

DAVIS

Worry creased my brow as I walked back to my... house. If she were half as happy as I felt right now, I could never tell her the truth. My eyes watched the road before my feet, stopping at a heads up penny. My hand reached down for it, but it halted half way. Stupid superstition, I scolded myself. That's how you got yourself into this mess to begin with... Joanie's face, the heart, winning. Like that penny would really bring me the luck I needed to be with Mel forever. Lincoln stared up at me as I straightened, leaving his face there for some wishful child.

MEL

The first time I truly forgot Mom was gone happened the next morning. When I woke up, I called, "Mom! Guess what?" I had to tell her the good news about Davis and me. Perhaps I sought motherly advice about the lost love situation, however misguided that advice would be.

"Mom! Mom, you'll never guess what happened last night!" I yelled down the hall as I pulled on a tee shirt over the only sport bra I owned.

Dawning my sweat pants and running shoes, I rounded the corner to the kitchen. Sunlight twinkled through the window above the sink, but no coffee mug, no Mom, no bottle of vodka, no orange juice. The accident, the ride in the hearse, the flowers all drifted to the surface of my love-filled brain.

My butt plopped into a chair as my emotions crashed momentarily. I was alone.

Searching sadly around the kitchen, my eyes rested on the freezer door. With Superman's X-ray vision, I clearly saw the Rocky Road ice cream sitting there. The smile returned and the bubble of joy grew again lifting me and my mood right to the pantry for some breakfast. Davis' golden brown hair poking up in just the right places, neat yet not, his crystal blue eyes, and his lips pressed to mine saved me from my well of pity.

I wasn't alone. And I at least wouldn't spend today alone!

I couldn't wait to tell the girls later!

Grabbing my brush from my dresser, I headed for the bathroom. Brush teeth, brush hair, pull hair back...I stopped. No bun today. A ponytails didn't pull as much.

It's probably cool outside, I told myself. I pulled my hair to the side and brushed the straight dark sections until they shined. Then I pulled it to the other side and repeated the process. When I threw it over my shoulder, the ends swept the middle of my back. I hadn't worn it in a ponytail in years, until last night before I readied myself for bed. Today, I felt like showing it off while I ran, as it was one of my best features.

Wandering through the house, turning the TV on and off, checking the time, I grew more concerned by the second. Maybe I had still been asleep when he came by. I hadn't fallen asleep until this morning, and then slept six hours, too excited to get a full eight.

At noon, I went to the door to look out and there he stood on my front porch. We had perfect timing! I just believed more and more that we belonged together each time we met.

"I was just about to knock," he looked at me as though running was the last thing he wanted to do. I know my face tinted pink. I had to look away.

"Sure, uhm, let me get my key," I reached to pull the key off the peg next to the door, but then thought of my estranged grandparents and their paying the bills. I stepped out the screen door and pulled the interior door closed behind me.

"You look...really good in sweatpants," his half smile drove me crazy. Running was now the last thing I wanted to do.

"Uhm... thanks?"

"Maybe we better just run," he nodded, as if reading my mind.

"Yeah," I turned away. "Where to?"

"You take the lead. It's your neighborhood."

I peered down the street one way and then the other. "No car again? You sure you have the energy to run?"

DAVIS

"Oh, yeah, I rode over with a friend on his way to the hardware store." I already hated lying to her. Good thing she was looking away.

"Oh, okay, well, the law of nature states that most right handed people go instinctively to their left when walking or running, so let's prove the law wrong! And let's see if I can keep my feet under me on the way!" she referred to her near spill the night before.

"Sounds good." I stretched along side her in the yard and we jogged off to the right.

The swing of her ponytail reminded me of another opposite ponytail, Joanie's. I knew now that I had only been infatuated with the idea of the love her and Franky shared. Mel was the girl I loved, the one that would make my life complete. We had goals and we could share those goals together, through thick and thin. I still needed Joanie, but only to help me out of the mess that would tear Mel and me apart should she find out the truth.

As we ran, our feet matched strides, though she was about half a foot shorter than me. Our breathing came evenly, also matching. In through the nose, out through the mouth, our shoes making little sound with each step we took. Uphill, downhill, through alley ways, over the bridge on the river through the park, down the winding paths around the small lake where swans, ducks and geese bathed contentedly while old people filled the benches, one old couple holding hands as they fed the begging, quacking ducks crowding at their feet.

That's where Mel slowed down. Just behind the old couple, at the drinking fountain.

"That's what I want when I get old. I want to sit on a bench in the park holding hands with my sweetheart," I raised my chin in their direction.

I felt her eyes on me as she circled, slowing her breathing without stopping her movement.

Was she my sweetheart for life? I would bet on it.

"You want that? We could have that now, if we had some bread," she teased.

I couldn't help myself, running over to her I grabbed her around the waist and swung her playfully in a circle until she broke free, running a few paces before my arms found her again and we fell over on the ground, rolling downhill the opposite direction from the lake and out of view of the passersby.

She squealed as we rolled. I laughed, my deep voice contrasting her high pitch.

She couldn't believe I tackled her, the surprise evident in her eyes, her rounded mouth.

I couldn't believe I had either. But there we lay, side by side on our backs, our hands barely touching, laughing and huffing, trying to catch our breath, staring at the blue sky through the branches of trees above us.

"Where did you come from?" she joked.

"I could ask the same of you," I rolled onto one elbow, bracing my head with my hand so I could see her perfectly flushed cheeks.

"I asked first. I can't believe we've never met before. I never noticed you before. Who are you?"

"A Greek god. Just call me Zeus."

"A little full of yourself, don't you think? Besides, Adonis might be more appropriate," she smiled playfully, making me want to take her right there.

Control, I told myself.

"Ah, yeah, Adonis. And you wonder why I'm full of myself with girls telling me things like that? Well, only a god could make a goddess like you fall for him." I raised a brow, picking leaves from her fanned out hair. She bit her lower lip as her eyes moved to my chest.

She stared shyly into my eyes for a second, blinked, then planted her hand in my chest and pushed me over to my back. "You're so corny!" She shouted as she jumped up, taking off at a run. "Race you!" her ponytail swung over her right shoulder as she threw the words over her left.

Sitting up, I stared after her. I had been ready to kiss her before she raised the challenge. Why did corny work for Franky, but not for me?Â

Shrugging off the intensity, I sprinted to catch up to her and then surpass her.

She kicked into higher gear. "That water fountain!" she pointed.

We were neck and neck before the run reminded me of the county race and I pulled up, afraid to win, afraid of what would happen as we neared the finish.

She paused at the water fountain near the parking lot, "I win! I win!" She bounced in circles, her arms punching the air above her.

I jogged in place before her, "Yeah, you win." I was happy to let her. Winning wasn't everything as I had discovered that night so long ago.

"You had me back there. Why did you pull up?" Her perfectly arched brows rose in question.

A wispy smile touched my lips, "Cramp."

"Sure. You were just afraid I'd get angry with

you if you won!"

"Nah. I like a good race. Hey, let's get some lemonade or something." My head jerked toward a lemonade stand.

She plucked her empty pockets out.

"I'll get it. We can sit in the shade and cool off before we walk back."

"Gee, Adonis, are you sure you have time? Haven't you already spent your four months with me?" She rolled her eyes.

"Just go find a nice shade tree and I'll meet you there, Aphrodite."

"Ah!" She laughed, but she moved to the largest, most secluded tree in the park, stretched a bit, and sat beneath its outcast branches cross legged.

"Drink slowly," I cautioned her as I handed her the cup.

"I know. I ran track a year, but I didn't care for the competition. I like to run for fun." She sipped her lemonade, then found a level spot on the grass to set the sweating cup. I held my cup in my hands, as much to cool my sweating palms, as to face her so I could take in her every movement.

Resting under the shade of an oak tree wasn't

exactly the image that played in my mind. This was the girl I would marry. I didn't know how, or when, but I would marry her. I envisioned us rolling around in the grass on the other side of the knoll, my hands finding places on her body that made her want more.

She'd dodged that one.

"Didn't your mother ever tell you it's not nice to stare?" She peered up at me from the corner of her eyes.

"Yes, but my dad always added that it was alright if I was staring at a beautiful woman."

"Oh, my! You know, corn is the hardest vegetable to digest."

"Might be, but that's the truth. My dad told me that while he stared at my mother when she got onto me for staring at someone else."

She giggled at the confusion of that sentence.

"Your parents sound like good people." She lifted her cup to her lips again, the straw touching the perfection my own lips desired to touch again.

"They were the best, and they loved each other. I always swore that when I fell in love, my marriage would be like theirs."

"Hmm, hope you find her, 'cause, honey, I am

far from corny!" She threw her head back, eyes lifted toward the tree top, leaving her fair neck open for my lips and the next thing I knew, the salty taste of her recently sweaty neck filled my taste buds, contrasting the sweetness of the lemony drink. She moaned as my lips moved up her neck, to her chin and found their home on her full, sweet, citrusy mouth.

Another moan escaped her throat traveling into mine, rattling my tonsils and traveling down, down, down.

Her hand roamed the back of my neck, caressing softly.

Mine slid from her neck downward, to her shoulder, down, pausing briefly at her breast.

My body filled with heat of desire as her finger slid beneath the collar of my tucked in shirt and pulled the collar out, at which time she dumped the ice from her lemonade down my back making it arch and create a funnel allowing some ice to slide right into my pants.

"Aye!" I leaned back onto my knees, pulling out my shirttail so the ice could fall freely to the grass behind me.

"You need to cool down, Adonis!" She stood up,

stepped around me and threw away her cup in a nearby trashcan.

I jumped up and followed, like a little lost puppy that she had just hand fed.

Yep, she was definitely my future wife!

"Okay, okay. I guess I was moving a little too fast, but, I don't know— life's short?"

"Nice try. We hardly know each other. Look, I'll maybe forgive you if we have a real date." She let her hand glide along a tree trunk.

"Okay, movie?"

"Popcorn?"

"Sure, Gobstoppers, milk balls whatever you want." Her in a dark theater... that's what I wanted.

"Really? Okay."

"Can I walk you home, or are you too liberated for that?"

"You better walk me! You copped a feel!"

She loosed a long laugh, music to my ears. I was afraid I had screwed up moving too fast. If there was one thing I didn't want to mess up, it was the love we could have together. Of course, I may not have a choice in the matter anyway.

Standing on her front porch, feeling like an

idiot, I stumbled with the wording to tell her I'd be back in a few hours. I had to stop by a sick friend's house to visit.

She stood before me, free strands of hair falling about her shoulders, a leaf still stuck in her ponytail. I reached over and plucked it out, dropping it to the porch. "So, I'll see you later." I licked my lips hopefully. I wasn't sure whether to kiss her or not after the park, but she answered my question by lifting on her tiptoes and kissing me. "Later, Adonis."

I stared at the door for a few moments after she disappeared inside. The door swung open again, "You better go now. You don't want to be late for our first date!" She stared wide-eyed at me, then smiled her brilliant face lighting smile.

"I was just leaving." I nodded and stepped down backwards gracefully off her porch.

"Show off!" She shook her head, rolled her eyes and closed the door, again.

To Franky's, change clothes, and back in a couple of hours.

I missed her already.

21

MEL

"Seriously, I wish my parents had been more like yours!" I reached in for a handful of popcorn as we sat in the dim theatre during the previews.

I wondered how he really felt about my choosing a romantic comedy. I guess I had wanted to test him, see just how far his making it up to me would go. This movie worked its way to the top of my must see list when Mags told me about it, and we were going to go together, the four of us, but we hadn't gotten around to it. Well, I would rather see it with him, anyway.

He swallowed some popcorn, "What were your parents like?"

"Hm... let's see. My dad is a drug-addled idiot in rehab or jail all the time. My mom was a drunk who cared very little for being a mother. They did not love each other. They did not seem to love me. They loved each other's addictions." It dawned on me when I spoke of my mother in the past tense that he had spoken of his parents in the past tense, too.

I took a mental note to ask him about that later.

"You're mom was in that car accident, right?"

"Yep."

"Sorry about that." He stared at me a minute, bewildered, but I kept my eyes on the screen, "Well, still, they couldn't have been that bad! I mean, you're so..."

"Messed up?"

"No, you got it together. Bet you're going to college on scholarships?" his voice lilted in question.

It was like he read my mind, "Yeah, I was just going to tell you that. Full ride!" What would happen when I left? Would he wait? "Are you going to college? Where are you going?"

"Oh, I'm not. I mean, I planned to, but that kind of fell through. Things happened." His hand full of popcorn paused in mid air for a moment.

It struck me odd that my messed up life afforded me a trip to any college in the U.S. while his seemingly perfect home life hadn't.

"So, you work, then?" I changed the subject.

"Well, no, not really..."

My handful of popcorn hung even with his for a split second. My eyes opened wider. He spoke of his parents in past tense; he didn't work, and wasn't going to college. I guessed his parents had taken care of him financially. Not only was he to die for hot, he was rich? My second chance at life was looking pretty good.

"So, you're rich?"

"Uhm... no, not really."

I inhaled deeply and sighed, giving up. "You're a mystery, Adonis!"

"Not really."

"Now you're messing with me! If you say that

again, I'll punch you!" I teased.

"I'd rather you kissed me." He puckered his tempting lips as the lights went completely down, leaving only the movie screen reflection glowing in his face.

"Uhm... no, not really!" I shook my head, turning my eyes to the beginning of the film.

His arm slipped around my shoulder, pulling me toward him, causing a tingling sensation of warmth from head to toe. His hot breath filled my ear, "Don't worry, I know you have almost a full soda over there, and it's loaded with ice," he whispered, sucked my earlobe between his lips, gently took it between his perfect white teeth, then let it go and turned to face the screen.

After that, I couldn't keep my mind on the movie. I squirmed in my seat, trying to focus, get rid of the heavenly tension; I gobbled popcorn, I shifted, but all I could think about was his hand resting easily on my shoulder, his lips and teeth playing with my earlobe, and whatever else we could be doing right now besides watching a movie.

I wanted more, but I didn't want him to know I wanted more.

For almost two hours, I imagined what we could be doing in that dark, nearly empty theatre.

"That was a surprisingly good movie!" He nodded as the lights came up. I stared dumbfounded at the screen.

"What's the matter? You didn't like it?" He prodded, a smug smile playing his lips.

I turned to him, disbelieving he sat and watched the entire movie without making another move on me. Looking into his face, that smug smile, his playful eyes, I knew. I was going to marry this guy for sure.

Walking back to my house at twilight, the first star peeked at us in the quickly darkening sky. The streets were quiet for a Saturday night. He held my hand in his, lifting it once in a while to kiss a knuckle. The little park we stopped at the night before beckoned to me. We sat on the swings beneath the stars and talked.

"You're parents are gone, then?" I asked quietly.

"Oh, yeah," he nodded. "A few years ago."

"I'm sorry." I pressed my feet against the ground to start the pendulum motion of my swing. "They were young, then, like my mother," I added.

"N... yeah, I guess so. It's okay, though. I've

adjusted." He sounded so sad. I wished I hadn't brought it up.

"Do you still live at home, in their house?"

"Most of the time I stay with my best friend."

"Oh!" I thought of Kathy and moving in with her now that Mom was gone. I still wasn't sure what would happen there. But I guessed Lester and Paula would take care of me, from the looks of it.

"Are you okay, living in your mom's house alone?"

My feet dragged the swing to a stop, and I looked up at the stars, then rose to my feet. "Yeah, I guess. It gets lonely, but as you see, I'm hardly there. I can make it 'til college starts."

He quieted after that. I shouldn't have said anything about college. I took a few steps away from the swings and he followed, putting his arm around my waist and turning me to him. "I'll wait for you...if you go away." An odd, sad look filled his face. I couldn't figure it. Why had he looked that way?

"You mean 'when I go away.' I'm glad you'll wait. I wish you could go with me," I breathed.

He lowered his lips to mine. He hadn't kissed me since he left earlier, and I had waited all afternoon for him to do so; I held on and wouldn't let him stop until neither of us could breathe. I wanted so much more, I wanted him, but I couldn't risk my plans. He'd said he would wait.

He squeezed my hand tightly as he walked me home and he kissed me again on the unlit front porch.

"Tomorrow?" I hoped.

"No, I have to stay with my friend tomorrow. His time here is almost over."

"Oh, Davis, I'm so sorry."

"It's all good. I might see you Monday, at the school. I have to find my other friend. It's kind of important."

"Oh, okay. 'Til Monday." I kissed my fingers and pressed them to his lips. His hand covered mine and he kissed the same spot on my fingers. Placing my hand on his heart, he leaned in and kissed me goodnight, a soft, short, gentle kiss, but surprisingly full of more desire than the hot moist one preceding it.

Floating into the house on a cloud, I went straight to the phone.

No, this was something I had to tell the girls in person. I'd tell them Monday.

Sunday passed and I thought of him all day, trying to focus on schoolwork was hopeless, so I left it undone. I wandered, ran, bathed all the while hoping he would just drop by the house, but he stayed true to his word and didn't show. By midnight, I tired from the daydreams of him and drifted into night dreams.

Grabbing my book bag, I headed out the door, just as Kath's car horn blew.

"Kath! Guess what?"

Kathy still seemed a bit sad this morning. It must be the flowers. I really needed to clean that up. "Picking you up has become such a habit, I imagine when we graduate I'll still automatically drive here."

It was true, except the morning of the accident; she had picked me up for school since the six months wait time after getting her license.

Her mood was bringing me down, again. I wondered if she blamed herself for not picking me up that morning. She couldn't help having a flat tire when she woke up, and it certainly wasn't her fault Mom was gone. Hoping to bring her mood up, I told her all about Davis.

"Oh, Kath, he's incredibly hot! I'll point him out today if he comes by the school! Or, maybe introduce you. Kath, he's the best thing that's ever happened to me in my life!" The bubble grew again. A sweet smile formed as her sea green eyes looked through mine and into my heart; though a quiet sadness filled them. She was so emotional that sometimes it annoyed me.

Rolling her car into a parking space, silence followed us into the school.

Nobody stood near our lockers; my eyes roamed the halls in search of him. Funny, though we had met and spent nearly the entire weekend together, I still couldn't focus on anything but him! Shrugging off his apparent invisibility, I waited for Mags and Ruthie so I could tell them the news. I had stayed up pretty late and a yawn caught me. Maybe something bad happened to his friend; maybe he slept in. He didn't have to be here at eight, after all. He really didn't have to be here at all.

Figures, I wore my new outfit and left my hair down this morning after brushing it until it glistened.

He would show up. I knew he would.

The girls ambled up, frowns clouding their usually exuberant personalities.

"Mags, Ruthie, guess what? That guy I saw last week showed up at my house Friday night," I began when they joined Kathy and I. We all must have been up late. They remained quiet as I rambled on, barely focusing on my words. Maybe they were angry with me for not staying over Friday night. I reasoned how I would feel about it if I were one of them as the four of us meandered to class. That's when I spotted Davis at the other end of the crowded hall.

"I'll be in class in a minute. I just saw Davis. I'm going over to see him."

As I drew closer to him, I noticed his face pinked with anger; he looked down at a beautiful girl with strawberry blonde hair and flashing green eyes. Dressed in retro clothing: white blouse, rolled up jeans and sneakers, she argued up at him. The urge to move closer took me further away from the girls and class.

Was she the one he had become so pained over?

Was he breaking up with that girl?

Or was she his Persephone? The other woman?

I supposed the other woman would actually be me, as I was apparently the new one.

Leaning my back against the end of the nearest row of gray lockers, her sharply whispered words barely reached me through the then thinning voices in the hallway, "I saw you leaving her house Friday afternoon, and then you two were at the park Saturday, Davis! Did you tell her the truth? Did you tell her about us? What are you waiting for? You have to tell her, Davis!"

"Just shut up! It's none of your business!" His words cut through the varying voice levels around me.

"It's wrong, Davis, and you know it! You know what will happen if you date her! It's not fair! You cannot fall in love with her! You're supposed to…"

"Shut up! I'll do what I want, when I want! It's none of your business! I've never been in love…until now! Never!" he emphasized.

"Really? What about Joanie?"

"No... this is different. She's the one," his voice quieted, seeking to stall any further argument. "Have you seen her? Joanie?"

"No, but this is wrong and that girl has to know the truth about you and Joanie! You have to tell her!"

The conversation ended with tears clouding my vision.

He was seeing someone else.

He intended to date me and her at the same time.

My crystal heart cracked into a crimson rain as I pushed my way through the hall of bodies making their way to class.

"If iths too good to be thrue, then it iths," Mother's slurred words followed me past my first period classroom. Never having listened to her failed attempts at motherly advice before, I don't know why I chose now to remember those particular words, again.

23

DAVIS

My sister always butted into my business. It pissed me off so bad. It was like she came all the way here just to stick her nose into my love life! So what if she'd seen us at the park. She wasn't going to change my mind. Nothing would change my mind. If we couldn't spend all eternity together, then we would spend what time we have together.

I thought I glimpsed the back of Mel's head as I

stormed away from my sister. Mel's swinging dark hair hung down the middle of her back just above her perfect hips. She hadn't pulled it back, for me. I was sure of that.

Certain Mel saw us in a rant; I pushed through the zombie like bodies wandering before class and I tried to catch up with her.

She rounded a corner and disappeared into a crowd of giants, the basketball team. Pressing close to the wall, I slipped past them. I would just have to catch up with her in the afternoon and explain...

No, somehow I knew if I waited to talk to her, I would lose her. She would shut down.

The only reason I knew is because that is what I would do. Bricks had been going up since I first saw her, and this weekend, some had fallen. If I were to have seen her in the situation she just saw me in, my wall would be all the way up.

The problem was, what would I tell her when I caught her? I couldn't exactly tell her why my sister was yelling at me.

What then? I wasn't even sure I could tell her that who she saw was my sister because then I might have to tell her about the one thing that would certainly ruin our relationship, and I loved her.

I knew that I loved her, but she wasn't ready for that particular truth.

And if I couldn't tell her the truth, how could I tell her about Donna or Joanie?

More importantly, what was I going to tell her about the things she might have overheard?

Lies spun in my head, weaving and smothering every other thought in my brain.

I was never a good liar. My parents always saw through me.

My heart crashed into my stomach. A lump closed my throat. I was going to lose the girl I truly loved because I couldn't tell her the truth. Memories of the weekend floated in and out of my thoughts. I had to find her.

MEL

What a jackass! I couldn't believe I fell for that charm! I needed to scream... run... punch a wall! Fighting my way through the basketball team just made me angrier. I wanted to talk to the girls. I needed some advice. Surely this exact incident had happened to one of them.

Not Mags, but maybe Ruthie or Kathy.

I couldn't talk to them; I couldn't' talk to

anyone; I felt like a fool. He played me. All weekend, all the feelings that had built up between us, they were all moves. There was nothing about him that was special! He was just another guy that couldn't get enough from one girl!

Tears blurred my vision, and for the first time in my life, I exited the glass doors at the end of the hall without a thought for my grades.

Well, what was another day of makeup work? Considering current events in my permanently screwed up life, I'm sure my teachers would understand. The principal, too, she would just wave it off.

I would return tomorrow and hopefully he wouldn't be here. If he was, I would dodge him. He could spend the rest of his life looking for me and never find me. "I'll wait for you if you go," his words echoed between my ears. "Ha!" I nearly screamed in the courtyard.

Well, I had the whole rest of my life to get over my stupidity.

DAVIS

Her beautiful hair waved this way and that way as she exited through the double doors. Like a salmon, I pushed upstream of the swarming crowd in the hallway. I had to stop her.

Think, my brain yelled.

My voice traveled the distance of the courtyard as the fresh air hit my face, "Mel!"

Mid step, she paused at the center, surrounded

by windowed classrooms where students readied themselves for class.

"Please," I begged her. "Please, stop! Don't throw away the weekend because of what you think you heard. Let me explain, Aphrodite," My voice softened, whispered upon the breeze.

What was I going to explain?

MEL

My lids closed when his soft plea reached my ears. He had to call me that, bring back the memories I had pushed fruitlessly away beyond my warning signs. My heart told me to turn, but my brain told me to run. Somewhere in the pit of my stomach, I knew he would come after me, hunt me down. He wasn't about to let me go. I resigned myself to listen to his sad excuses, but they were not going to sway me. His charm would not bend me.

* * *

DAVIS

"You? Skipping school?" I asked her playfully, trying to lighten the mood.

"Well, there's a first time for everything!" the cold words stung my face like a strong north wind carrying sleet, and she turned to glare at me.

"Look, I understand what you're thinking, but, that girl in there? She's... uh, she's..." I glanced away, then back into her eyes, "my sister."

MEL

He wasn't lying. Living with Mother had made me a master lie detector.

DAVIS

* * *

"The one from the mall?" her face softened.

I nodded pleadingly.

MEL

"Oh." That was all I could say to him. A flush of embarrassment crept from my neck upward. That answered that question, but what about this Joanie? Was she the friend he was looking for last week, the one he loved?

"You don't really want to skip school?" His half smile.

"No," I sighed, rolling my eyes to the windows next to me.

"Can I walk you back in?"

"If you tell me who Joanie is," I crossed my arms, stood my ground. I don't think he expected that. I wouldn't let it go, though. He would have to tell me sooner or later why he was looking for her.

"Can I tell you later? It's kind of a sad story and I really don't want to start the day like that. Do you? It's not what you might think."

His eyes held no indication of my suspicious feelings.

He was happy I had stopped, listened, and recently allowed him to take my hand.

"Okay," I relinquished.

"You're so beautiful," he whispered into my hair as he guided me through the door, sending a shiver of warmth through me. I exhaled; the anger, the hurt, and the self-pity flowed out into the now empty hallway. The touch, the tingle, of his warm hand in mine relaxed me and cast an effervescence of joy about me, until my bubble was pierced by angry green eyes at the end of the hall.

"Don't pay any attention to her. I'll deal with her later. Come on. I'll walk you to class," he leaned into me, pulling me closer, leading me away from the sister who hated me, someone she didn't even know.

Those light jade eyes had reasons I didn't understand. Perhaps the hate I saw was not directed at me, but at her own brother who had somehow betrayed her, me. What was it he should tell me? What was it that wasn't fair?

It had to be him because I couldn't understand

how she could hate me, but then again, some girls bred hatred for others? People did hate people without knowing them. They did it all the time in school, and out of school. That was a part of human nature I never understood. Everyone deserved a chance to be liked.

I vowed when his soft lips touched my forehead that I would find out all about their conversation later that day; my questions would be answered.

As it happened, I didn't have the chance.

DAVIS

$\mathcal{I}$ had a huge problem, now.

I had to keep my meddling sister away from Mel. If Donna found any time to be alone with Mel, she would tell her and I could very easily lose Mel, forever.

Even though that very thing could happen without Donna's help, I couldn't let it happen that way, and not right now.

If Mel and I could only be together for this short time, then I wasn't about to let anything stop it. But more importantly than that, I wanted to find a way for us to stay together forever.

I loved her with my entire being.

I knew that.

And I had never been in love before. The infatuation I carried for Joanie had been nothing like what I felt for Mel. I would die…

If we had to run to stay together, I would persuade her to run with me.

I would find a way.

After each class ended, I was there waiting for her. I walked her to every one of her classes. She briefly introduced me to each of her friends, disappointed that they weren't more excited for her, "Imagine Mel with a boyfriend," green streaks had said to the quiet one, Kathy, I think was her name. I thought it was kind of a rude remark for a friend to make, but I may have misunderstood.

We spent lunch together, alone in the courtyard, whispering our love, though her words came hesitantly because of all the questions she carried about earlier.

As much time as I spent trying to protect her,

prevent her from running into my busybody sister, the one place I could not go with her was the Girls' Room, and that was the one place my sister could go. Donna bumped into us in the restroom hallway after lunch, although I was pretty sure it wasn't an accident. She arched her brow at me, smiled and tried to follow Mel through the door. I reached for Donna's arm just before she could slip through the door and I managed to drag her into the hall.

"What do you think you're doing? Let go of me!" She stormed, attempting to tear her arm from my grip. My strength always outdid her, though. She couldn't get away from me.

"Leave her alone," I threatened through gritted teeth. I stared firmly into her angry eyes.

"Really, what do you think you can do to stop me? Nothing. Nothing, nothing, nothing," she smiled smugly.

She was right. There was nothing I could do to stop her. She could do whatever damage she wanted to do to me and my relationship. Arguing wasn't going to make her stop.

"Please," I begged her. "Just let me spend the time I have with her. I will tell her, but let me do it. Give me the chance to tell her myself."

She caved.

I saw it in her face.

She was my sister after all. She couldn't stand seeing me hurt, and she knew her meddling was hurting me now. But, I also knew she was just looking out for me. What I was doing was really dangerous, for me and Mel. What future we may have could be gone in a flash, probably would be anyway.

"Okay," her eyes softened as she turned toward me, "you have one week. If you haven't taken care of this before next Monday, I will. It's not fair to her, Davis. You might ruin any chance of resolution she has left. And you know what that means!" She warned. "I can't let you do this to yourself, Davis. I will not lose you because of her. And, besides, you really need to help me find Joanie!"

It was the only choice I had.

She was right. The week was ours and then...

"Thank you. I know you're just doing this because you love me, and I will help. I will," the corner of my lip rose.

"Oh save your charm for eternity, brother," she started for the door as Mel returned.

"Hi!" she stuck out her hand, "I'm Donna," and

she actually smiled, a friendly, warm, open smile. I hadn't seen her smile that way since the night of the last race, the county championship.

"Uhm... Hi?" Mel limply shook her hand.

"I'm Davis' twin sister, but, not the kind of twins that look alike. You're Mel, right? It's nice to meet you. Have a great week! Excuse me," and she slipped past Mel through the half-opened door.

"Uh... okay... that was weird..." Mel's naturally shaped brows rose.

"Yah, she's a little ticked off at me right now. And then, you know? The whole twin thing. She's really protective. Come on! You're gonna be late!" I entwined my hand in hers and led her to her next class.

We were safe until next Monday.

I could at least spend the week with her.

27

MEL

That had to be the strangest encounter I've had with another girl. My mind filtered through the conversation, jumbling it with math problems, neither for which had I found a solution. Storming home this morning would have accomplished the same results as I had achieved so far today in my classes.

If my thoughts weren't on Davis, they were on

his all too jealous sister and her abrupt, emotional, and weird introduction, not to mention this Joanie and Davis' urgent need to find her.

I really wanted to talk to Mags, Kath and Ruthie. Whenever I thought about Davis, no matter how he smoothed over this morning's episode, a nagging sensation of danger imposed upon me.

I didn't trust Donna at all. Have a great week? What did she mean by that? Nobody says that except a salesperson, or teacher, sometimes. Her sudden change of feeling stumped me.

I waited by my locker after the last bell rang, hoping the girls could give a few moments of input.

Unfortunately, only Kath showed up, still in her quiet mood. I shared my concerns with her on the way to her car, but she just shook her head once in a while.

It must be senior-itis. All the teachers talked about it. Seniors were changing more the closer we came to the end of the year, growing more irritable, distant with the other students and teachers.

I guess I was too; I just didn't notice it as much.

We walked through the parking lot, Kath in the

lead, amidst hoots and hollers from loaded buses. Kathy pushed the unlock button on her key ring and we climbed in. She wouldn't even look my way. "Kathy, are you angry with me or something? You, Mags and Ruthie all seemed a little strange today, a little distant. What's up?"

"I am so hurt, Mel! And angry, maybe. Yes, angry! You left us. You weren't there Friday night for our usual sleepover. I have never been so angry! I want to hit something!" Her palm smacked the steering wheel.

This wasn't like Kathy, the quiet one, the gentle one. She never expressed anger, not really. She had a golden heart and took situations in stride. She'd been acting really different lately. Remaining quiet on the way home was my only option. I apologized to her and then clammed up. She'd already frozen up on me, anyway. Pushing down into the seat, trying to disappear, I stared out the passenger window the entire way home without another word.

When Kath stopped in front of the house, I exited the car to find Davis sitting on my front porch.

He jumped up and took my book bag as Kath

sped away. I had hoped to spend time with both of them together, let them get to know each other, but she wasn't really in the mood anyway. I wasn't either, now. Everything was changing so fast. In exchange for my bag, Davis handed me a red rose.

"What are you doing here?" Again, no cars graced the curb outside the house. "How did you get here before us? Oh, that's right! You don't have to hang around until the last bell and you don't have a job. You know, some would call you a bum, a loser."

My nose wrinkled with curiosity.

"Probably, but some don't know me and you do. Am I a loser?" He glanced down the street as Kath's green sedan turned the corner. "Or am I not?" He slid his free arm around my waist, turning me into his kiss. Glad his arm supported me as my knees jelled, I wrapped mine around his neck; the lone flower draped over his shoulder and touched my cheek.

I wanted to stay like this forever, but I knew it was impossible, unless...

DAVIS

No, I couldn't think that, couldn't wish for it; I had already caused Franky enough damage throughout his life.

What I did in my stupid youth tormented him every day. I couldn't hope for that to happen, no matter how much I loved Mel. And I did love her. Moist tongues entwined; flushing heat rose; impatient hearts raced, and I grasped for ways to tell her what I was supposed to tell her.

It would devastate her and I didn't want to see her beautiful face filled with pain and dread at seeing me.

My heart sank at the thought of scaring her.

Lifting my head, ending the longest kiss I had ever been involved in, I looked into her dream filled eyes. This is how I wanted to remember her. All I could hope for was her falling so in love with me that after I told her the truth she would still love me enough to kiss me this way. I wanted the last time I saw her to be just like this, and that last time would come too soon.

* * *

MEL

"What's wrong?" For a brief moment, his eyes filled with pain. I could feel it, physically, and it scared me.

That danger sign flashed in my mind again. I had never been so empathetic with anyone, even the girls. My guard was always up, but now the brick wall of defense I had built all these years crumbled and his fear of losing me planted itself in my heart. In such a short time we had become that close.

How had this happened?

When?

"Will you tell me?"

His eyes shifted and then found mine again, "Yes, but not now. I only came by for a small piece of reassurance that you still felt the same about me after meeting my sister. Now, I have to get to my friend's house, the one who's really sick. I'll see you soon, maybe at the school tomorrow, if I make it up there?"

"When? When will you tell me?"

He sought an answer in the sky, almost a prayer, and then pulled me tighter. My head rested against his shoulder, his cheek on my head, "Soon, very soon," he softly kissed the tip of my nose when I searched his eyes. He held my hand as I moved up the porch until our arms stretched too far away to hold on. I couldn't let him go.

Whatever he had to tell me was going to ruin us.

Why did I feel that way?

I didn't even understand how I knew it, but I did. When he told me, he feared he would lose me. Could he have done something so horrible that I would never want to see him again?

The worst deeds filled my mind as we said goodbye.

"I love you," I whispered making him return to me.

And I meant what I said.

I knew I loved him and I doubted that anything he could have done in the past could change the way I felt.

He squeezed me and a warm tear dropped into my hair as my own fell on his shirt.

His voice cracked with pain, "I love you, too."

DAVIS

Tuesday, when I dropped her bag below the mantle, the urn caught my eye. I stared at it a moment and then turned away.

I couldn't leave her alone again after this week, after professing our love to each other.

I followed her into the kitchen where her amazing body stood in front of the refrigerator, her head hidden behind the freezer door while she rummaged for a snack, cold steam billowing about her.

"Ice cream?" she leaned back to see my response and held a carton of Rocky Road up for my perusal.

"That's my favorite! How'd you know?"

"Actually, I didn't know. It's mine, too."

She jerked open a sticky drawer and grabbed two spoons. After slipping by, she led me into the living room, plopped down on the couch, and turned on the TV. I accepted the offered spoon and the open carton. My head shook with laughter when she turned on the TV and pressed the channel select button until she found the show she wanted to watch.

"What's so funny, now?" her elbow poked me in the side as I handed her back the carton and put my free arm across her shoulder.

"That you watch this stupid ghost show! Rocky Road, yes. Ghost show, no. I guess we can't have too much in common."

"Well, have you ever really watched it? It's very interesting."

A spoonful of ice cream quieted her as she watched the opening, waiting for my answer. I watched her for a few moments, eyes affixed to the TV, chewing chocolate-coated nuts and marshmallows. Who would have thought that eating ice cream could be so sexy? I could do this every night for the rest of the week.

I could do this forever.

"Not really," I finally responded. "It makes me laugh. I can't get past the ghost portrayals."

"Well, it's actually pretty good."

I settled in next to her to watch the show, my left arm across her shoulder, but still couldn't understand anyone's attraction to this so-called reality show. People wandering the earth in search of ghosts wandering the earth? Seriously?

My right hand spooned ice cream; my left hand found strands of her hair, twirling them gently around my fingers and letting them fall. When I laughed at the show, she pulled the ice cream out of reach, turning her body so I couldn't get my spoon into it.

"Hey! Everyone's entitled to their own opinion! I mean, what makes you a ghost expert? Have you ever seen a ghost?"

She tilted her head toward me, but didn't look at me, like she really had to think about that question. "Yah, everyone's entitled to their own opinion, but if it doesn't agree with mine, you don't get ice cream! And, no. I don't think I've ever seen a ghost. But then, I don't have the right equipment," she nodded to the show.

I half smiled at her and she caved. "Agh! Fine, Adonis!" She brought the carton back into reach and leaned into my shoulder.

Even in the glow of the TV, the only sound in the room for several minutes, I would spend eternity this way, my arm around her as we shared our favorite ice cream.

"Last bite," she declared as the show neared its close. She turned the carton to me.

"You take it."

"No, guest takes it."

I nodded, dipping my spoon into the carton. "You were wrong. That's the last bite." I declared as I brought spoon to mouth.

"Well, thank you," she flushed spooning out the other half.

The carton empty, the show over, a tense silence filled the room. "I need a napkin. You?"

"Nope."

She started to rise, but I held her in place.

"I'll get it."

Pulling her to me, I kissed the chocolate film from her lips. The empty carton clunked to the floor; spoons clinked and silenced into the dingy carpet. I knew an end would come to this euphoria engulfing us, the heat flowing from my searching mouth to my toes. I longed to hold her forever, but Monday would come too soon.

"Can I stay here this weekend?" I paused long enough to ask, and then returned to her warm lips. She hesitated a moment, breaking the next kiss I emphasized, "I mean, nobody's at my place, except Donna; nobody's here…"

"Well, the only possibility of someone coming over would be my grandparents. They stop in sometimes. But, I'm not ready for…

"Me, either. I just want to be near you as much as possible." The desperation filling my voice made her frown.

"Because of what you can't tell me yet?"

"Let's not talk about it now," I breathed onto her pouting lips. "Can I stay?" I punctuated the question with another kiss.

"Yes," her whisper tickled the fine hairs bordering my lips, sending a shiver throughout my body.

"You can stay now," she suggested, "and every night. Do you need to go home, get some clothes? I'll go with you."

"No, I have to find someone, and I'm kind of staying with my friend this week during the day. I'll get clothes tomorrow morning." My lips drew down upon hers again.

My hands roamed her body seeking secret places that increased her desire.

Suckling her fair neck, one hand roamed the heat-filled skin beneath her lacy shirt, a sensitive side of her breast, the hook at the front of her bra while her back arched into me and whimpers of wonder slipped into my ear. I felt her hand grasping my hair and returned my mouth to hers in a hunger-filled kiss that left us both panting.

MEL

$\mathcal{I}$ don't know why he couldn't tell me what was bothering him, but whenever the subject came up, I felt like shutting down.

I was certain it was bad, really bad. I knew it would likely tear us apart and that was the last thing I wanted, since we had just found each other. How could I let him go now?

Comforted in his arms, warmed by his gentle

kisses, I vowed to not take this time for granted. If this were my last day on earth, what would I do?

After the quick passing of my mother, the changes in my life, it became a fight to make the right decisions. I wanted to live for the moment. I wanted to do whatever I wanted, but I also wanted to remain grounded in my desire fulfill my plans. Just how important were my plans, now?

If this were my last day, college wouldn't even be an option. I would spend my last day with him.

When he asked me if he could stay the weekend, I had to make it clear that I wasn't ready for that, but I said it as much for myself as for him. I needed to slow down, but I didn't want to. We had so little time together that I wanted to do everything we could, even that.

If this were my last day, I would make love with him.

It did cross my mind once that maybe this was just a ruse to get me to sleep with him.

Guys did that kind of stuff.

Maybe he was like that too.

But I kept replaying the conversation I overheard with his sister, and I kept reviewing the feelings I was empathetically receiving from him now as he kissed me in places I had never been kissed.

And then, there was his sick friend. He seemed as vulnerable as me.

No, something big awaited us after the weekend. Something his sister wanted him to tell me, but I didn't care and didn't want to think about it now.

It wasn't just a ruse. My heart knew it wasn't. My heart knew we loved each other.

So, should I or shouldn't I? When would we get another chance to be together if we were going to be torn apart?

I couldn't count on that and do something to screw up my entire future, though. It was a risk I couldn't take with him, or anyone, right now, wasn't it? I had to stick to my plan no matter how confused I became. I had to stop him soon.

Just having him here, now, being in his arms, feeling his warm, soft lips on my neck, his hand working its way toward the most sensitive areas of my body after sharing ice cream, just feeling loved, that was enough, wasn't it?

If I never got the opportunity to make love with him, I would be satisfied having what we have now for the rest of the time we had together.

When the passion between us overwhelmed me, as dark settled around us, I wanted to pull away from him, remind him that unlike him, I needed to go to bed, but when his lips touched my stomach, moving slowly upward, my back arched to his trailing tongue and all thoughts left me.

Abruptly, he forced himself to stop.

Later, leaning against the door, after he left with his desire, I touched my lips, my neck, my stomach, the places he so passionately kissed moments before, and I felt my own lips tighten in a smile.

I sighed and headed for my room. That night, I dreamed of Donna and Davis. She shook her finger at him ferociously, pointing at me and then back at him. A beautiful pouty blonde with a bouncing ponytail sauntered up to them, threw her arms around Davis, and kissed him on those lips.

When I awoke the next morning, my pillows scattered the floor where I apparently threw them in my sleep.

30

$\mathcal{The}$ next two mornings, Kathy seemed a little more like herself. She must have forgiven me. She even seemed a little happier. She blared her radio and sang with me on the way to and from school, like we used to do, our favorite music filling the car. I thought maybe I could get her and Davis together after school, but she drove away and he didn't show up until later, only staying for an hour. The closer the weekend got, the more pained our meetings became for him. On Friday he showed up right after Kathy dropped me off, as if he were waiting for her to leave.

Lester and Paula had apparently restocked the ice cream and cleared the flowers from the front porch. I had been watching the flowers die off, one by one, as the days wore on, promising the next day to pick them up, carry them to the trashcan, but I never seemed to have the time or desire to do it.

Davis pulled me to him first thing when we closed the door.

"You cleaned up the porch," he spoke into my hair as we swayed in each other's arms, the intense heat rising to challenge us.

"Nope. Lester and Paula did, I guess. Hungry?"

"For you," he joked, tilting my chin with his hand to kiss me, "Maybe later. What do you wanna do tonight? It's Friday and I'm staying," He raised his brows, nodding to the bag he had dropped next to mine.

"Okay." I glanced shyly at his bag, remembering how heated we had become on the couch the other night. For some reason the news that he was definitely staying made me very nervous.

It was what I wanted, wasn't it?

I guess I feared what I might lose, a part of

myself, or the love we had developed.

"Don't worry, I'll take the couch," he smiled knowingly. Raising his hands in the air he added, "and hands off. You probably sleep with a glass of ice cold water next to your bed, anyway!"

"Okay, Adonis!" I laughed, "but the couch isn't really all that comfortable."

"It'll be fine. You know, I am actually a little hungry."

"I'll see what Lester and Paula dropped off."

"Lester and Paula? Why do you call them that? They're your grandparents, right?"

"Yep, or so I've been told. I haven't seen them in some time."

Sticking my head in the freezer felt really good at that moment. It balanced out the warmth spreading through me as he caressed my sides with his strong hands. The thought of him sleeping in this house after our last night alone, the way I felt when he touched me, I even had to inhale the icy air in a deep chilling breath.

"Frozen pizza?" I called out just before I felt his hands slip around to my stomach, searching for the hem of my shirt, his chin on my head.

"Uhm... sure. Pepperoni."

"Pepperoni it is." I slipped from his grasp and pushed some buttons on the oven.

"Playing hard to get, Aphrodite?" he raised a brow.

Oven preheating and pizza on pan, I turned back into him.

"If you only had twenty four hours to live, what would you do?" I couldn't believe he had just asked me that very question, as if he were reading my mind. I know he saw the surprise in my eyes, because his face relaxed into a smile.

"Why? Are you going to kill me?" I opened my eyes wide, feigning a terrified damsel, relieving the tension between us.

"Hm... hadn't thought of it, but maybe."

I punched him in the stomach and ducked out of his arms.

"Well, if you're going to kill me, I want a fair chance!" I yelled as I ran into the dining room and circled around. When I came into the living room, he blocked my path. I grinned.

"Seriously, Mel. What would you do?"

He really wanted me to answer his question.

"Why are you asking? Do you have the money to take me to Paris? Rome? Australia?"

"Is that what you would do if you had twenty four hours to live?"

His sincerity sobered my playfulness, causing concern.

"Do you only have twenty four hours to live? Is that the secret? Is that what you have to tell me? Is that what will tear us apart?"

He glanced down, and then met my eyes again. "No," he replied uncertainly, then he repeated more assuredly, "No."

"Is it me? Do I only have twenty-four hours to live? How would you know that if it were true?"

"No. I just wondered. I guess, you know, with my friend being sick, it's just something I've been thinking about. You know what I would do if I only had twenty four hours to live?" his eyes tried to seduce me into biting, though I knew his answer already.

"Cool it, Adonis, or I'll have you sent to the underworld early!"

He laughed, "Then you already know that I would spend my twenty four hours holding you closely and…"

His face was so serious.

I didn't want to be serious about this.

We only had a short time together as it was, and that probably would happen, but it scared me to think so.

My eyes smiled as I moved toward him. I wrapped my arms around his waist, pressed my head into his chest. "Whatever I would want to do would most certainly have to be with you."

He smiled again. His arms wrapped my shoulders and warmed me.

"After the pizza, let's go for a walk," I poked my chin into his collarbone, rolling it up and down. His shoulders bent forward, trying to escape the pain.

"That's probably a good idea, but only if you stop doing that."

I needed to get out of the house before my security wall crashed around me and gave in to bodily satisfactions. Just being this close to him, knowing he would be here all weekend, him admitting out loud what he wanted, maybe even expected, made me want to do things I'd been arguing with myself not to do.

DAVIS

Steam flowed from the oven when the pizza pan was removed, but I'd lost my hunger by then. Being this close to her made me want to take her hand and lead to the one event in life that I hadn't made time for. One look at the steaming slices changed my mind about staying, "You know, the pizza will be here when we get back," I suggested to her.

"Yep!" She nodded, desiring escape, too.

MEL

He entwined his fingers through mine and led me out the front door. I felt strange. I never turned down a pizza, if not just one slice. Love would be good for my diet, maybe.

My head pressed into his shoulder as we walked. I paid no attention to where we were, as long as he was beside me. Like a slow dance, bodies pressed together, I let him lead me, eyes closing from time to time.

The contrast between the cool air and our warm bodies tantalized me. Invigorated, playful feelings moved through my being.

If this was love, I couldn't believe I had passed it by so many times. Having never reached out for it, grasped its fine wings while it fluttered about me, made me sad. But then, if I hadn't waited, I might have missed Davis. I smiled up at him and he pressed his lips to mine, a brief, love-filled, expression of what I felt at that moment.

We walked until dark fell, and the night grew chillier. I loved walking with him, running with him, being with him.

I loved him.

Without a care as to where we were, I let him lead me.

When he stopped at an older home and turned to face it, it pulled me from my trance.

Sadness flowed from his eyes down to his warm, soft hand wrapped in mine, and reflected on my own face. We truly were one, as I'd read so many times in those silly love novels. I guessed they weren't so silly after all.

"Is this your house?" I ventured, hoped.

The lonely presence of the old Victorian hovered in my peripheral vision.

Turning my eyes to its darkened features, its lifeless shrubbery, and its solemn shield of depression filled me with pain. The varying lost shades of grayness brought a streaming tear to my cheek, its cool traces a momentary shift in my senses.

A single window held light, its flickering indicative of candle flame.

Certainly this was not his home, but if it were, it would explain the anger of his sister. This house had to be a hundred years old, or more. The houses around it reflected newer, brighter, and happier places.

A vision filled my thoughts, this house in its youth, acres of sprawling land spread beyond the streets of my little town. Small children played in the front yard, chased around the wrapped porch. Flowers filled the beds surrounding its foundation, strength in beauty. My mind produced the happiness in the old home that I so desperately needed to see.

I did not want sad.

His statuesque features remained solid while I

waited for his answer. After moments of quiet reflection, he sighed, "No."

"Why are we here, Davis?"

"My best friend lives here. I want to introduce you to him."

"Do you know what time it is? Is he even up?"

The flickering candle whisked through my thoughts answering for him.

"He doesn't mind. I visit him all the time, whenever I feel like stopping by. Come on," through the wrought iron gate he led me up the cracked weedy walk.

"Maybe not tonight. Maybe we'll come back tomorrow," he suggested, stopping at the door, turning away.

"Okay, let's go back to my house."

I really didn't want to go in.

It was so gloomy, so sad. It made him solemn, and I wanted us to be happy.

DAVIS

$\mathcal{I}$ hadn't intended to take her there, but as we walked my feet followed the familiar direction. A block away, an idea sprang into my mind. Perhaps if they met, perhaps if he saw how happy we were together, it would change him, change the outcome, change Monday.

I loved them both.

I had to try.

If it would allow me to spend eternity with her, it was worth a try, wasn't it?

I couldn't let her go.

She was incredibly sad, because of me. I didn't want our only days to be this way, but if it worked, it wouldn't be our only days. We would be together forever. I had never experienced real love, true love, and I wasn't ready to let it go when I had waited so long for it.

It was a mistake, bringing her here. I knew it when I stepped onto the porch, felt her sadness grow as we drew nearer to Franky's house.

"Yeah, not tonight. Maybe we'll come back tomorrow," I suggested.

"Okay," she answered. I could tell she didn't want to go in.

Monday was only two days away.

If we left now, would I bring her back tomorrow?

What if it worked?

What if it didn't?

I looked deep into her eyes, and she into mine. Without speaking the words, she stepped onto the porch and pulled open the screen door.

We entered the dark house, but I knew my way

so well that I easily led her through the foyer to the stairway and upward. As we neared the bedroom door of my old friend, Donna burst through.

"No, not tonight!" she whispered harshly. "You should be…"

"Hello, Donna." Mel surprised me with her calm greeting.

The determined look of longing in my eyes doused my sister's flame, "Fine! Go ahead! It's not like it'll help anyway! But you know what could happen if it works," she left the doorway and silently stomped down the stairs.

I turned to Mel, a simple smile of optimism on my face. Perhaps it would work, and to my favor.

She hesitated at the threshold, shyness, fear of the unknown penetrating my hope.

At the side of the old brass bed, I whispered, "Hello, Franky."

Old eyes flickered.

A grunt broke the gloom.

It was now or never.

"Franky, this is Mel… Amelia. I love her, truly love her."

"Hi, Franky," Mel touched the wrinkled hand, accepting of him, making him instantly an old friend.

Frantic eyes searched beneath flickering lids.

My free hand rested on his receded gray hair.

"Now I know," my tear spotted his turned back sheet, "how you felt about her... Joanie. I understand now Franky, how much I hurt you. My heart would rip in two, like yours did, if I couldn't be with Mel forever."

The damp circle on his bedside sheet grew. A few more strokes on the graying head, a silent cry of redemption slipping from trembling lips, and I led Mel from the room.

In the darkened hallway, I leaned against the flowers shaded by gray and let the guilt loose in heavy, shoulder shaking sobs.

Donna had been right.

MEL

$\mathcal{I}$ had so many questions, but now wasn't the time to ask.

What about this Joanie, this secret, Franky's girl?

What about what Donna said, what wouldn't help?

I had never seen a guy cry before, and the fact that Davis was the first guy I had seen cry hurt me twice as much.

I lay my cheek on his back, letting my arms circle his waist, and held him until his breathing stilled. I didn't know who this guy was, or why Davis called him his best friend, but somehow I understood that our future together depended on this man who seemed closed up in his own comatose world.

My roaming eyes found closed doors at the end of the hall and I wondered if family lay sleeping behind them.

Were Donna and Davis this poor man's only visitors? Where was his 'Joanie' that Davis referred to?

Davis pushed away from the wall, wiping his face with both hands before turning to me. "I'm sorry."

"It's okay. Let's get out of here... do something fun," I suggested.

"Yeah, let's do that."

I led him down the stairs and out the door. The night much quieter than it had been, much later, we strolled down the empty streets to the park, our park. We sat on our swings, our hands clasped. A bittersweet silence filled the air around us. I had to break it. We had to open the air so we could enjoy our time together.

"Who was that, Davis? Why do you call him your best friend? He's so old. He has to be as old as Lester, at least."

"Yep, he's old. And he is my best friend, always has been."

My brows furrowed. Puzzled I waited quietly for him to continue his explanation.

"When I started driving, I got into street racing, drag racing? I loved the feeling of flying past trees, mountains, houses. I felt free, like when you swing, or we run. My dad taught me to drive when I was nine, so I could handle a car by the time I got my license."

I began to wish I hadn't asked. The tone of his voice, the choice of his words indicated an ending I no longer wanted to know about. I wanted to close my ears to this conversation immediately. Perhaps it was my recent car accident, the loss of my mother, I don't know. I didn't want to know the rest of this story, "Let's go back to the house, watch TV, eat pizza... be happy," I pleaded, tugging at his hand.

His eyes sought the pea gravel at my feet,

moved to our hands, still clasped, and found refuge in my defensive features.

"Not yet. Let me finish. I have to tell you anyway. You have to know. It's the beginning of what I have to tell you before Monday. If I don't tell you, Donna will."

I didn't want to know. My head shook frantically.

"Mel!" he squeezed my hands gently.

His face blurred through my tears. I refocused to his words.

"One night, I hopped in my souped up '57 with a winning night in my windshield. I had worked all summer on the motor in that car, making it the fastest motor in the neighborhood, in the county. I'd paid for it with my own money and I was going to make it back ten times over by winning just that night alone."

His eyes stared off into a past time, a lost joy, a lost innocence. I knew it would end badly, but I listened because he wanted me to.

"It was pitch dark as I backed out of the driveway. My parents were finishing dinner. Donna was up in her room, grounded, or so I thought.

"When I reached the park to pick up Franky

and Joanie, this park, my sweet ride pulled up right over there to that curb," my eyes followed his finger, "Donna's head popped over the seat. I yelled at her, told her I was taking her home, but she screamed back at me that we were the same age and I had to let her tag along or she would tell Dad I was racing. I was so mad at her. It was the first time I felt like hitting her. She pleaded with me to let her ride along. Franky reminded me that we didn't have time to go back.

"I was racing the county champion on a mile of straight away. I'd been earning this race all through the summer, win after win. Determined to be the county champ, I drove off with my sister, my best friend and his girl into a world of heart pounding danger.

"I found out that night that Franky and Joanie were getting married. She was pregnant. Life was changing so fast, you know? You would think fast would be okay with me, a racer.

"I watched Donna and Joanie as they ran across the raceway, Donna's strawberry blonde ponytail flouncing from side to side, Joanie's golden one matching it, and they joined the truck full of kids headed slowly down the road to the mile marker.

They would be the first to view the winner. They would get out at the finish line and form a human side border to cheer their winner to the white spray painted line. It was amazing to me, to watch my friends' faces in the headlights as I passed, hear the hoots and yells of their lit up faces, the blurred circles of their mouths as they yelled, 'GO, DAVIS!'

"I shook my head and smiled at Donna and Joanie as they waved excitedly from the back of that truck."

His face relived that moment of his life, and I couldn't hear anymore, didn't want to hear anymore.

It wasn't making sense, but it was making sense, and I didn't want to know.

I couldn't take any more pain, his or mine. I hopped off the swing, clasped his face in my hands and kissed him, hard. I would rather give myself to him right now, throw away my future, than hear the end of the horrible story he told me. I knew how it was going to end.

His lips remained firmly closed to my probing tongue, but didn't resist for long. When he kissed me back, I felt safe, safe from the pain he was sharing. I wanted to spend this time being happy. I wanted him to be happy. I pulled him from the swing to the cool ground below. Kissing madly, we rolled together to the grass. My hands sought his dark hair, his neck, his tight shoulders, and moved quickly down his back to his waist.

I didn't want to know anymore. I just wanted the Utopian joy we had shared together this last week.

His hands pulled my head to his, but he quickly broke the kiss, his desire filled eyes turning firm while he looked down at me, stroked my hair spread out in the grass.

"Not now, Mel. You don't want this. You just don't want to hear about Franky."

"No, I don't! I want to go back, back to the house, back to normal, back to happiness!" I yelled, trying to push him off of me, trying to escape his firm grip on my face.

"We can't go back, Mel. We can only go forward and I have to tell you."

"But not 'til Monday. Let's just wait 'til Monday, please." Tears streamed from the corners of my eyes, dropped through my hair and to the cool grass below.

"Mel, I love you." He kissed me tenderly,

calmed my tense body. "There's so much I have to tell you by Monday. There's so much I want to do with you by Monday." He stroked my hair, searched my desperate face, kissed my nose. "Let's go back to your place, eat some pizza. Then I'll finish. Okay?"

I nodded and he pushed himself up off the ground, gripped my hands and pulled me up, brushing grass from my back, pecking it from my hair.

His arm crossed my shoulder and wrapped my waist as we walked. I leaned into him, feeling his love flow from one side of me to the other, spreading, the wild fire from our first night together returning to my body.

Perhaps we could forget his past and just move forward.

DAVIS

Time passed quickly on this side, and I had to tell her before it was too late, but I couldn't rush a budding cocoon into an angelic butterfly. If the butterfly didn't exit its home at its own pace, it would die. You couldn't dig it out of a warm, soft nest and expect it to live just like you couldn't crack open a half formed chick's shell.

Mel wasn't ready, and neither was I.

I had tried to rush because of my guilt, and it almost backfired on me. I would have to wait until her curiosity about Franky brought us back to the story.

Returning to her kitchen reminded me of Goldilocks and the Three Bears. Our pizza had been sliced and two pieces taken. Mel shook her head, a bag of groceries sat on the table.

"Lester and Paula," she said. "They always come over when I'm out."

"Your grandparents?" I frowned at her continued expression of them by their first names, but hoped their visit wouldn't ruin our weekend.

"My grandparents, I think. They always leave groceries. They have since I was little. It's their way of caring for their only grandchild, I guess. They're paying the bills, too."

"Are they here?"

"Nope. They never stay. I never see them. It's like they're ghosts or don't really exist."

"Oh." Though I was relieved that they wouldn't interfere with our weekend, I was alarmed at her grandparents' distance toward her.

"It's okay. No reason to feel bad. I've gotten used to it, to them, the way they are with me." She shrugged it off, grabbed the pan and turned for the living room.

"Drinks?" I called to her.

"In the fridge. There's a carton of cokes."

"Got 'em!" I let the refrigerator door swing shut, shook my head again at the bag of groceries, and joined her on the couch. "No more ghost shows, please," I pleaded.

She laughed in response, but didn't reach for the remote to turn the TV on. "I don't feel like watching TV anyway." She bit the pointy end of the piece of pizza in her hand. I popped her coke open and handed it to her.

"Thanks!" Her lips turned up at the corners.

We ate in silence, slurping soda between bites. I felt the question before she spoke it. She was going to ask about Franky.

"Why is your best friend so old? He has to be about ninety, right? I mean, I've never known a teenager to be best friends with an old person. And, why was your sister there when we arrived?"

It wasn't what I expected her to ask, but it was a start.

It didn't matter, anyway. To explain, I had to go back to the race. And in order to keep talking, I had to get her interest up first. I had to tell her what happened.

"The night of the race, I killed Joanie and Franky's unborn child."

The rest of her pizza dropped from her hand, fell to her lap. She turned to me, "Joanie? Franky's Joanie? Their baby? How? No, wait! Why would you tell me that?" she screamed. "That's not even what I asked you!" She fumed, her face filled with anger.

"I hit her with my car, accidentally. And she wasn't the only one, but she was the love of Franky's life and I broke his heart because of a stupid race! He never got married. He never lived his dream with her. He loved her so much. They were so happy, so much in love. Like us.

"I hoped he would wake up tonight, meet you, forgive me, and then die so we could stay together." The words rushed from my mouth in a jumbled mess of syllables.

"I don't even know what you're talking about! What was an old lady doing out there while you were racing? How could a woman that old be pregnant? That's stupid! How did that happen?" She rose from the sofa and flew to the mantle, fuming, then she whipped around, expecting answers. "I don't know why you're telling me this. It's the past. You said we couldn't go back, only forward. Why do we even have to talk about this?" She ranted, stomping through the living room, not wanting to hear me anymore. It was so difficult to continue, to retell the events of that tragic night that led up to this one.

"She was only eighteen. She was as beautiful as you are. She was cheering for me."

I fell into memories of that night, Joanie's face as the front tire blew out.

"Eighteen? What kind of sicko is your best friend? Jeez, Davis. What are you talking about?"

My mind turned to the present, her confused face, her defensive stance. "He wasn't a sicko. He was my best friend and he was my age when he and Joanie were together."

I let that set a moment, hoping she would figure it out, hoping I wouldn't have to tell her.

She calmed down. She did the math. "Davis, that man hasn't been nineteen for sixty or so years. What's wrong with you? Why are you acting like this? You're scaring me again." She returned to my side, her sneaker squishing the piece of pizza into the carpet.

"It was forty-nine years ago, not sixty something. He was nineteen, forty-nine years ago when I ran over his fiancé with my car, killing her instantly, and Donna, too."

"Davis, you're nineteen years old... wait a minute! Donna? Your sister? The one at school? The one at that house? You're not making any sense, Davis! Do I need to call somebody for you? Are you okay? Are you... sick or something?"

"Yes, Donna, and no you don't. I'm perfectly fine."

It was now or never.

"Davis, that can't be. We just saw Donna at Franky's house. Are you sure you're okay?"

"That's not all, Mel. That's not all I have to tell you. The accident didn't just kill Joanie and Donna. My car flipped, threw me out, and bounced back onto the road like it was possessed. When I hit the ground, my neck snapped."

She looked at my neck, scanned by body, then her eyes turned to my own. "What are you telling me, Davis?"

I took her hands in mine, caressed them tenderly with my thumbs until she relaxed. She tried so hard to deny the truth she knew.

It was now or never, and it had to be said.

"Mel, I've been dead for forty-nine years. I've been waiting for Franky's forgiveness for forty-nine years. I've never experienced love, until you. I was going to go to college. I was focused on my future, just like you—" I gripped her hands tighter, but she pulled them free.

"Mel?" I begged as she stormed from the couch again. She was reacting exactly as I had feared she would.

"You're crazy!" She yelled, shaking her head in disbelief. "Get the Hell out of my house!" She stomped away from me to her room, slamming the door behind her.

I had hoped I'd never hear that tone, see that anger in her face. "I knew it! I knew this was too good to be true. I felt the danger of this relationship yesterday. This is ridiculous!" The house shook with her words, bounced as she paced in her room. And then laughter, the most hysterical laughter I've ever heard rose from her lips to the ceiling, traveling throughout the dimness surrounding me.

* * *

MEL

I returned to the living room, "You're making this up because of the ghost show! Oh, Davis, this is such a good prank!" I laughed, uncertainty cracking the sound. I held my stomach, bent forward in hysterical laughter, rose and turned toward the sofa where I had left him.

He was nowhere to be found.

I searched the kitchen, the dining room, opened the back door.

He was gone.

Swinging the front door open, I hurried outside and down the sidewalk. He couldn't have run far; I could catch him, if I could see him. At the curb, the streetlight's glow left circles of light below, and he didn't pass beneath them in either direction. "Davis!" I called both directions.

If it was a joke, why would he leave? It had to be a joke, though, I reasoned.

Returning to the house, lost in replay of the past moments, the pain filled words he had spoken to me, I timed it. My rattled brain stepped through the motions, realizing I had to turn the dead bolt when I ran after him. He couldn't have left so quickly and locked the door.

The spare key!

Hoping, yet not, that it still hung on the peg next to the door, I ran to the living room. If he was crazy, and had my key, I'd need to leave fast! Maybe he was going to kill me!

Glancing at the peg that held the spare key only confused me more, and reinforced his story. The key was still there, the door had been locked, and he wasn't in the house, but just to be sure he wasn't playing a joke on me, I searched it again anyway, flipping on all of the lights and then turning them back off.

DAVIS

She had thrown me out.

I couldn't believe I hurt her like that.

Once again, my sister had been correct.

Knowing where to go, I vanished. I could do that now. She knew about me, though she didn't believe it. I should have waited until tomorrow to tell her, but the closer we got to Monday, the more chance I stood of losing her, but if I had waited, we would still have two days.

It wouldn't have been fair to her. I had already taken too much away from her by not telling her sooner. I had been selfish, wanting what I couldn't have, what I could never have. My only choice had been to tell her and hope she loved me enough to believe me.

And she didn't.

Creeping up to Franky's bedside, I rested my arm on Donna's shoulder. "What are you doing here? You should be with Mel before she leaves Monday!"

"I told her," my eyes blurred the way Franky's had the night of the accident. If it hadn't been for Franky, I may never have figured out that I was dead. "She kicked me out."

"Oh, Davis, she just needs time. Did you tell her everything? She should know everything." Donna hugged me around the waist. I rested my head on hers and stared down at my best friend.

"No. She didn't give me a chance."

"Davis, you have to tell her. She loves you. She needs to hear it from you."

"She doesn't love me, Donna. If you had seen the look in her eyes, you wouldn't say that."

"I did see the look in her eyes, brother. She looked at you the way Joanie looked at Franky that night, like he was some Greek god. You are meant to be together."

I chuckled at her Greek god comment.

"What?"

"Nothing. She called me Adonis."

"Well, I just don't see that, Davis!"

We both laughed. "It was meant to be," she whispered.

"But how? How can I go back there? She was so angry."

"Remember that time Dad stopped at a bar with the neighbor? After work? He didn't come home until midnight, and he was drunk off his rocker?"

A smile touched my lips remembering how funny he had been that night.

"Remember Mom?"

Mom was furious. She grabbed handfuls of his clothes and chucked them out the window. She wouldn't let him in the room and told him to sleep on the lawn with his clothes.

"Think about it Davis, about the look in Mom's eyes that night. Would it compare to Mel's? Mom and Dad stayed together, until the accident tore them apart."

"Yeah, you're right. Mel looks at me like Mom looked at Dad. But, being dead hardly compares to being drunk. It complicates our relationship a little."

"Complicates it, or makes it easier? Give her some time. She'll call your name and you'll go back to her, because that's what you both want."

I don't know when my sister had gotten so wise. She wasn't wise when she died. She wasn't patient. Right now, she sounded just like Mom, felt like Mom. She even resembled Mom a little.

There's a lot I've missed being dead at nineteen. Love was something I hadn't shared with anyone.

I'd found the woman I loved more than anything, but had no idea how to make it work, or whether it even would.

34

MEL

Pacing the living room wasn't helping me believe his words.

It couldn't be true. Ghosts were things searched for by people who helped them "move on."

He couldn't be a ghost! I could feel him, his arms around me, his lips on mine. He was warm, passionate, gentle.

People can't feel ghosts, can they? I would be

shivering, like in that stupid show. No wonder he thought the show was stupid. People apparently didn't know the real secrets about ghosts.

No, wait. How could he still be nineteen?

If I could see him, feel him, taste him, wouldn't he age?

Crap! Mom would freak out if she knew I was dating an old man! He had to be as old as Lester!

This entire idea was ridiculous! I laughed deliriously.

Grabbing the TV remote, I switched on an old movie, a romance.

Thoughts of Davis holding me, us rolling in the park, swinging while holding hands, at the movies in the dark, all drifted through my mind like clouds in the sky. In all those memories, during those times, people would have thought me crazy talking to myself, yet nobody even noticed us. I don't recall anyone pointing and laughing. So many questions filled my thoughts.

Had he somehow taken me to the world of the dead?

And what about Franky? He was alive, but on his deathbed. How could he be in that plane, dimension, or world and this one at the same time?

Confusion, restlessness, fatigue led me to my room where I plopped on my bed face first and cried on and off until sunlight pressed its way into my room.

I'd had love, and now I didn't. I had felt love and it was fake.

Sleep wouldn't come to me; hunger left replaced by nausea; tears dried out.

I loved him so much!

But he was ghost!

A ghost that traveled between my world and his taking me with him. That was the only answer.

The urge to run, work off the anxiety and anger, the feelings of foolishness, took over and in moments I dressed, stretched and left. I would go to the park, find the lemonade stand owner, see if he remembered Davis, my Adonis.

I didn't know why that was so important to me, but crazy as it might seem, I missed his touch, missed his love.

How could this possibly work?

How could we have a future together?

Ten minutes after leaving, I ran through the park, the sun fully risen, ducks, geese and swans already beginning their tour for bread. The lemonade guy kept his stand at the other end, so without stopping the burst of energy filling my legs, in another minute I waited for him to open.

"Good morning! Can I help you?" he smiled broadly.

That was a good sign, right?

"Do you remember me? I was here the other day with a guy, about this tall?" I held my level hand six inches above my head. "And, well, very good looking. He got two lemonades, and brought them over there."

"Oh, yes, the young Adonis," he nodded.

"A... Adonis?"

"Oh, I don't believe that was his real name, of course. He said that is what his girlfriend called him."

"But, you do remember seeing him?"

"Certainly. And you, too, Aphrodite. You sat right over there, beyond that knoll, under that tree," he frowned for a moment, certainly wondering about my mental state. Then his head moved slowly up, and slowly down. "Ah... poor girl. You don't know... you had a fight?"

"Yes, sort of." I was terribly confused now. He had seen us both. Yet, nobody paid any mind to us.

Nobody had even spoken to us. "Thanks!" I called as I rerouted my run for home.

Knowing where Davis had gone was easy, finding it would be difficult, especially if I were in one dimension and he the other. I knew he had left here and gone to Franky's, but the night he led me there I was blinded by love. I would never find it. Racing up and down the streets of town, I tried retracing our path in my memory, but it wasn't any use. Franky's house was as much a mystery as Adonis himself. The phone book would hold no useful information as I didn't know Franky's last name. Besides, what would I say if someone answered? Is Davis there? Yes, I know he's dead. They would hang up on me thinking me crazy. Of course, they may not. The lemonade guy had seen us. My feet weakly took me home. I had no idea how to contact a ghost who could be seen by people.

I showered, changed clothes and still no resolution for contacting him presented itself.

Would calling his name work? Could he hear me? How did ghosts communicate with the other world? My mind drifted to that stupid show, the weird gadgets people designed to "talk" to ghosts.

Now I laughed at the unrealism of it! It certainly was starting to look like a pretty dumb show, now.

If I called Davis, would he show up? I had called to him last night at the curb and he hadn't returned.

I was losing my mind. That was the only answer for all of this. PTSD, Post Traumatic Stress Disorder from the accident had brought this all about.

But it was so real. Could hallucinations be that real?

I didn't know what to do anymore.

My mouth opened three times, forming his name, but nothing came out.

I kept remembering the hurt in his eyes before he left, the pain my anger and disbelief caused him. That look brought to life the pain that crawled from his hand to mine that night we walked. That was what he had thought about, telling me, losing me, that had hurt so badly.

He hadn't been crazy; I had. Crazy to throw him out, crazy to let go of my only chance at true love. I still didn't know how it would work out. What if he "crossed over" before I died? How would we have children? How could we possibly have a future? I had asked if he had twenty-four hours to live, not leave.

Monday! He'd told me we had until Monday. Monday must be his day to leave.

Was him being a ghost really so important now? So little time, and I throw out the man of my dreams. How dumb can I be for such an intelligent person? We had two days left, and then he would be gone. I had to find him, call out to him, get him back, somehow.

"Davis! Davis, I'm sorry! Please come back!" No matter what I said, he didn't return. No matter how loudly I called, nothing changed. "Adonis!" I tried.

Morning rolled into afternoon and no Davis. I lay on the couch, closed my eyes, and remembered.

All I would have left of him were memories. Fantasies of our past, present, future, played like a romance film in my mind.

In my movie, we married and I gave everything to him, embracing myself, as though my arms were his. I imagined his lips on mine, his hands roaming my body, seeking areas that brought me pleasure.

Tears slid down my temples as I lay daydreaming about him, about what I had lost.

"Uh...last time I tried that, you dumped ice down my back."

I laughed. I could hear his voice as though he were really with me.

DAVIS

Why was she laughing? I hadn't intended for that to be funny.

I went to her, bent over her, and pressed my lips to hers, kissing her hard and long. She put her hands around my waist and pulled me to her, but I braced my hands against the cushions to keep from squishing her into the sofa.

MEL

I didn't know at what point daydreams became realistic. I could feel Davis as though he were here, his lips on mine. But when the cushion sank in on either side of my waist, it became a little too strange, and I needed the dream to stop. I had to open my eyes, and when I did, his cheek, his ear, his hair filled my view.

He had returned.

His lips found the salty trails at my temples, and returned to mine.

DAVIS

I looked into her eyes, filled once again with the love I desperately needed to see, and smiled before I disappeared.

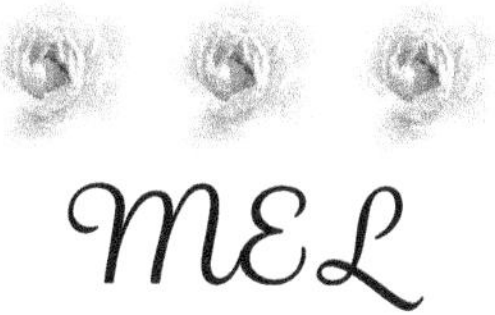

MEL

I don't know why he did it, but I guess he had to prove he was a ghost. Now I understood the door being locked last night when he left. He hadn't used the door.

"Davis?" his name fell out in a seductive whisper, "please come back. I know you're telling the truth."

I sat up, rested my chin in my hands, and waited. When he reappeared, he was kneeling before me, that heavenly half smile on his playful face.

"I had to go find some lemonade!"

Our laughter blended as one. "I'm so glad you came back to me. I'm sorry I got so angry last night. It's just...just so hard to believe. But... I love you and I want to spend the rest of our time together. I know we can't have a future after Monday, but we have now, right?" I peered down into his welcoming eyes.

"Yeah," he stood and my eyes followed him upward. His hands reached toward me, and I took them in my own, rising to him. Lifting our arms, he twirled me and pulled my back to him.

I felt his hands leave mine and slip around my waist, the warmth of his fingertips caressing the skin beneath my cami.

His chin pulled hair from my neck, replaced by his soft, moist lips leaving a trail that chilled me from my ear to the curve of my shoulder.

His cheek resting against my ear, he whispered, "If it all works out right, we can be together forever."

That would mean he would have to return to life, not cross over, or I would have to die. Did he know something I didn't know?

"Are you talking about Franky again, or are you really going to kill me?"

"Yes to Franky," a kiss on my ear lobe.

"But Davis, how will this work? I mean, I have so many questions, about Franky, this weird dimension thing you do, how our future will be if we are together for the rest of my life, and I guess beyond. What about our children? Would they be half ghost? I love you, but when you talk about the future, it only confuses and scares me."

"I still have so much to tell you, Mel." He turned me to him and kissed me, his tongue searching mine.

"But I need for you to listen, and not get angry."

"No more anger, Davis. I'll listen. It's just... you really scared me last night, what you told me about Donna, Joanie and you. I thought I was losing my mind." I shook my head over the silliness and immaturity of my response. His left hand caressed my right side as his right cleared the hair from my neck. His soft, warm lips found the curve on the other side of my neck, while his hands glided smoothly about my back, pulling me tightly against him. My head fell back, my lids closed and I tilted my face to meet his roaming lips, our bodies so close that are hearts beat as one heart in love.

"I love you," he whispered, his arms tight around my waist, mine around his neck, and when I opened my eyes, his face had taken on a serious look.

It no longer mattered.

I had to be with him, somehow.

Love had stolen my mind, and I would gladly give him my body. I pulled away before our searching hands delayed the clarifying talk we were about to embark on.

"Franky?" I whispered, wanting, yet not wanting, to know. "Why is Franky so important right now? What is it that he can do to help us in his state? How is it that he is in the real world, yet be a part of the ghost world where you can touch him and he can help us?"

His arms loosened, then dropped to his sides. "So many questions, so little time we have left. I would have thought you would figure it out by now. I thought all I had to do was tell you about the accident that took Franky's future wife and child, me and Donna. I hoped you would have seen it by now."

"Seen what? If Franky dies, you can take his body and live again? Is that why you have to find Joanie? Because she loves him and you have to ask her? Why is she hiding from you?"

"It doesn't happen like that Mel. That's not real. I can't inhabit another body and be alive again."

He turned away, stared through the open blinds a few minutes, and turned back to me, his hands stuffed into his front pockets.

He turned his eyes on me, and they were filled with sorrow. There was more he had to tell me and for some reason, I felt I should already know what it was, that somehow I should have learned it by now.

"I'm a ghost, Mel. I'm dead. I killed Franky's future wife and soon to be baby, which would have been a boy. I can't move on without his help."

"I know, Davis. You've told me that. Just tell me what you're trying to say. I won't get angry."

"I can't just tell you. And you won't be angry.

Think about it, Mel."

"Okay, people can't see ghosts, so that's where I come in, to help with Franky? But, if people can't see ghosts, then how am I able to see you, hold you, kiss you? It doesn't make any sense. Are Franky and I some kind of mediums or something?"

"Huh! That's why I laughed at the TV show. They got it all wrong. I'm a ghost, a nineteen-year-old ghost, and I'm in love with you. Franky can't see me, but he can hear me, feel me when I touch him. And you . . ." his eyes roamed over me from head to toe, "beautiful you? You make me feel so alive. It's as if I'm alive, or you're . . .â€ He couldn't bring himself to finish the sentence. His quiet, gentle words brushed my ears, but I refused to hear them.

"That's why we can't be together? You're a ghost. I'm alive. That's why Kath wasn't really all that excited to meet you? You need Franky's help for what? If he doesn't help you, you are stuck where you are? And when I die, I'll move on? I don't get it.

"And why can I see you? Because I love you? Why can't we stay together until I die and then for eternity?" Questions raced from my thoughts to my mouth stumbling upon each other. The truth was there, but I thought of anything, asked him anything to keep from speaking the truth.

No, the truth couldn't come out.

I forced it deep into the darkest recess of my mind.

No, I will not speak it.

"My being a ghost is part of the reason we can't stay together." His great patience with me flowed through his voice. He understood my pain in realizing the truth. "Another part is Franky and Joanie. I'm here, but only for as long as it takes for Franky to forgive me before he dies."

"And, he's dying now? This weekend? That's why we've only had this week?" I kept the conversation going if only to save myself from having to see it, having to let it rise back to the surface where I would have to face it.

"If he forgives me first, we can stay together. If he forgives me, then it means Joanie will come back for him and they can be together for eternity. He'll be with his true love. He'll be happy again. His heart will be full and heal, but if he doesn't forgive me..." He paced around me and I turned with him, as if spinning would help.

"You'll be gone Monday? Gone to wherever ghosts go? And when I die, we can be together like Franky and Joanie!"

"No, Mel. If he doesn't forgive me, then I stay until I can redeem myself." His eyes searched mine for the truth. He knew I had pushed it deep into the darkest recesses of my mind and he tried so hard to make it surface, but I couldn't. I couldn't let it.

"Well? Then we'll be together?"

"No, Mel. Think, Aphrodite, most beautiful of all. Think about the time we've spent together. You can see me, feel me, hear me, yet your friends cannot. You can see Donna, hear her, touch her? You don't love her."

DAVIS

This was so hard to do, but she had to come to the realization herself. I wasn't even supposed to go this far. Everyone learns on their own, but usually through the reaction of one who loves them. That's why she hadn't learned, yet. There was nobody there to love her.

MEL

This conversation was getting more confusing by the minute for me, but only because I blocked out the truth he led me to. I didn't want to understand what he was saying. I didn't want to understand how I could be in love with someone who wasn't actually there, yet I did, deep down with that secret waiting to claw its way to the surface of my thoughts, feelings, life.

No, I wasn't planning on going anywhere, but…

I looked into his eyes, his beautiful deep blue eyes that were trying so desperately to tell me something without words, so close the multi colored flecks sparkled into mine. When he disappeared again, leaving me staring at myself in the mirror, over the mantle, "Davis!" I called to him desperately. "Don't leave me at a time like this!"

His arms wrapped around me up from behind. "Look at yourself, Mel. Think."

Darkness crept through the window. We had been at this all afternoon but I wasn't even tired, or hungry. We hadn't turned on any lights in the house. A ray of moonshine reached through the clear window and trickled its way to the shining urn between me and the mirror.

This all began when you caused that accident, Mom! My mind yelled at her.

As if in reply, the moonlight played across the name plate, shining the letters one by one like a Ouija board spelling out its answer to a player's question. One by one the letters touched my eyes: A... M... E... L... I... A... K...E...R...

"What? Wait, that's not my mom's name!" I touched the urn. The moonlight played tricks. I shielded the urn with my hand, blocking the light, and yet could still see it. My name shown back at me, a shade lighter than the urn itself.

"No! No, something's wrong. This is a prank, right? This whole relationship is a prank. Everything, no, it's all wrong!"

DAVIS

I watched as her reflection faded in the mirror with her realization. She turned her face to me. The hardest part was over. She had let the truth surface that she was the one who had died in the accident, and her mother had lived.

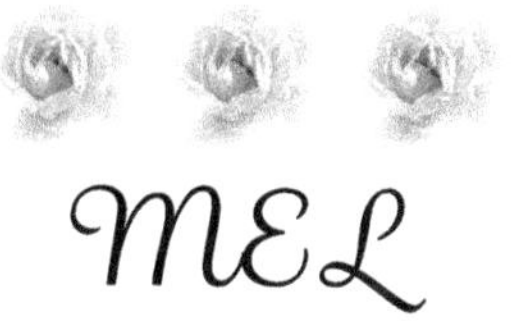

MEL

Davis frowned his sympathy down at me, his arms never having left my waist. "No, Mel, it's not a prank. It wasn't your mother; it was you. You... died... Mel." The words fell slowly to my ears.

I pushed away. "No!" I screamed at him and ran through the front door into the bright full moonlight. The door had remained closed. I hadn't turned the knob, pulled it open. Davis passed through it behind me, a sad expression filling his face as he watched me turn circles in the yard, my face lifted to the moon.

"Think about it, Mel. The day you saw me, your first day back at school, never noticing me before. Kathy's strange responses to you? Stopping here everyday was just her way of grieving for her best friend. Nobody coming by to see you, except your grandparents who are never here when you are... when you were with me, the people around us never noticing us, except the ones like us, the ones waiting." All the strange ideas I had been curious about flowed from his mouth as tears of disbelief streamed down my cheeks. Kath, poor Kath.

He reached his hand out to me, but I didn't want to take it.

"Please..." He pulled me back inside to my mother's room, the yearning moon blocked out by closed blinds and thick new curtains.

She lay there, my mother, on her bed, sleeping restlessly, tossing, turning, mumbling apologies to the darkness.

I turned away.

In the living room, Davis wrapped his arms around me again. "I'm dead," I said to the floor. "I had such big plans. I was top of my class. I was going to college."

"Your mother came home from the hospital,

and rehab, last night.
　　My knees buckled as Davis held me up.
　　I was dead.

261

DAVIS

Standing at his bedside, my arm around Mel, I spoke softly to him, hopefully. Family came in, left, returned without noticing us.

"Hey, old friend!" I sounded more chipper than the night before.

"Hi, Franky," Mel smiled, gripping his old hand.

A grunt, a twitch, flickering eyelids, same as always.

"I don't suppose we can help him along?" Mel joked.

I glanced at the extra pillow by his head.

"No." I was ashamed having even thought about it. "Remember the two lines on either side of the list. You'll go to the right. If I were to help him, I'd go to the left. We would surely be separated forever then."

"Well, I was just kidding, but we'll be separated forever anyway if he doesn't die before I leave, or if he doesn't forgive you, go with Joanie. He just has to forgive you," her head shook with despair.

"I know," I answered. "You hear that old friend? You'll have your revenge if Monday comes and we haven't resolved this. I can't believe that's what you want, though. I can't believe you would hold a grudge against me, against Donna, against Joanie, your one true love, for forty nine years to eternity."

A heavyset nurse with curly gray hair entered the room and placed a stethoscope to his heart. She nodded at a younger man sitting in a chair at the foot of the bed. The nurse shivered as Donna passed through her and stood at the other side of Franky's bed. The nurse reached through Donna and pulled up the old man's covers.

"A little chilly in here. This room has been so cold, lately! Would you like a blanket? Coffee?"

"No, thank you," the younger man replied, returning to the magazine he held.

MEL

"Who is he?" I nodded toward the man in the chair.

"One of Franky's closest nephews," Donna answered. "Though disturbing, spending so much time here, it has been interesting watching Franky's life play out. He never married, never had children, but he became very close to that young man, as if he were his own son," she added.

The nurse returned to the bed, reached through Donna and patted Franky's arm, "It's almost time, you poor dear."

"Uh! Rude!" Donna grinned at us across the bed as the nurse pulled her arm back through Donna's stomach. Donna had returned to her usual bubbly self for a moment, until she viewed her brother, staring down somberly at his old friend. "The nurse sounded promising. It's almost time?"

DAVIS

"Yeah, but it's still sad, watching him lay there, so ill, so heartbroken."

"We have to be here, you know. To see him before he disappears with Joanie. If he disappears with Joanie."

"I know." There was the possibility that Joanie had been in love with someone else.

Me.

So she's another who stood between us, Mel and me.

Mel leaned her head into my shoulder, a tear sliding down her cheek. The end of one's life was so heart wrenching, but to top it off with the end of our love was even crueler.

Donna's eyes softened and she reached across the bed to pat Mel's shoulder. "Keep hoping." She ran her hand over the extra pillow, pursed her lips, and looked up at me.

"No," I shook my head.

"It wouldn't matter to me. I have no reason to want to go right. There's nobody for me to spend eternity with."

"You have me, and Mel, Mom and Dad. No," I stated more firmly.

"Okay, I won't. But there won't be a Mel, if the end doesn't hurry and come soon. Look, you two should be spending the time you have left doing something else. I'll call you when it's close. Send you the twin signal, you know?"

"You're right. Don't do anything stupid," I warned, shaking a finger at her.

"I won't," she crossed her heart and smiled broadly.

Something told me she had her fingers crossed behind her back, though. Sometimes I didn't trust my sister.

Leaving the gloom of the house, I turned to Mel, "Paris?"

"Seriously?" her brows rose in interest.

"We can do whatever we want, go wherever we want, without restraint, without care."

"Will we find Joanie in Paris?"

"I don't know. We can look."

"I didn't look, but was her name on the list?"

"Yeah, just below Donna's"

"Why is she still here? Is she waiting for forgiveness from Franky, too?"

"No, she won't forgive herself for distracting me. She thinks my accident is her fault. We had a big argument...things were said."

"Why isn't she with Franky? Waiting? I mean, if they were so much in love, where is she?"

I sighed. Another moment of truth had arrived.

"Because Donna and I spend so much time with him and she keeps running from me.

"Once, I thought I was in love with her. Then you came along and I discovered that I always just wanted what Franky had with Joanie, not necessarily Joanie. After the funeral, I wouldn't forgive her for ruining my chance to win that night, for distracting me with the heart she drew with her index fingers. I wouldn't forgive her for risking what she had with Franky, for ruining my future. I had such a great future planned. I had been so careful to not let a girl keep me from my long-term plans. I didn't let any of them hook me into doing anything that would compromise my future. And then, there she was at the finish line betraying my best friend, or so I thought. Hindsight tells me she drew the heart to show me that she and Franky loved me, no matter what. I wouldn't forgive her at first, but now . . .

"I've realized how cruel I've been, keeping Joanie from Franky because my ego assumed her betrayal. She took off in a rage the last time she asked, and I haven't seen her since. Donna and I have looked everywhere, called out to her, sought her everywhere. I don't think we're the ones she'll respond to, though. It will have to be Franky."

MEL

"So, I guess I don't even have to ask, but you didn't win the race?"

Now that I knew the worst of all he had to tell me, the rest was a story I wanted to hear.

As we held hands and gazed at the Eiffel Tower, the lovers passing, stopping to take pictures of one or the other before the massive structure; as we strolled L'Avenue des Champs Elysées, as we viewed famous paintings in the Musée du Louvre, places I had always wanted to see, I guiltily hoped to unexpectedly be called away. I hoped to see Joanie, the blonde haired girl from my dream who planted a kiss upon my lover's lips. In my life, I never would have thought I'd want to be called away from Paris. Being dead was strange. As if something greater awaited, all of the dreams I held, traveling here and there, viewing the most beautiful areas in the world, no longer mattered.

"Actually, I did win. Well, my car won. After it flipped, throwing me from the window and landing on Donna and Joanie, it bounced back on its side and slid across the finish line. Of course, I watched from the fan line, standing there next to Joanie and Donna, wondering how I ended up beside them. They had not moved. It was strange, knowing my car was wrecked, but not knowing I was dead."

"Huh..." I contemplated. "It's still strange to me, knowing I'm dead."

A kiss on the banks of the Seine brought middle school art lessons to mind. "So you were spending all of that time at the school looking for Joanie because she would be a senior? She was eighteen, right?" I questioned.

He smiled into my eyes, "I hoped she would return to the school, go through the motions. And instead I found you, the love of my afterlife. I had always hoped to experience my first real love. I never had time for that when I was alive, though many girls tried. You should be happy you bagged me."

I pushed playfully at his shoulder. "You're so funny, Adonis! You should be happy you caught me! I had better things to do than fall in love."

I cut my eyes away from him and that's when I saw her, the girl from my dream, now a woman who looked like Joanie. "Davis," I whispered.

He turned his eyes the direction of mine, "Joanie," he whispered at first, then, "Joanie!" he cupped his hands to his mouth and yelled. The woman turned, her eyes filled with pain at seeing him, and she quickly ducked into a store. "Let's go!" I tugged Davis' hand.

"There's no point. She'll be gone before we get there. She's a ghost." His features grew depressed, pained.

"We can try, Davis. Let's just go into the store.

Maybe she's hanging around in there, watching us, waiting for us to leave here. Maybe she's waiting for you to find her, forgive her. Come on!" I dragged him behind me, his steps hesitant.

"Wait, stay out here. She doesn't know me. Let me go in and talk to her, if she's there." I pressed my palms to his chest to stop him from entering the opened door.

"But you don't know her, either. Are you sure you can find her?"

I blinked, turning my eyes to my sneakers, and then back up. "I dreamed about her, before I knew about my death. She hugged you, kissed you. I... I was jealous, but I know what she looks like. Stay here, please, just look like you're searching the street for her."

I entered the small touristy store casually, browsing the small Eiffel Towers, the Paris, France key chains, and the landmark watches. Softly I hummed to myself as I perused the gift shop items, the souvenirs, so I could find her.

And I did. On the other side of the shop, she did what I did, but her eyes wandered periodically to the window where Davis stood outside, looking past the citizens, who were trying to look past the tourists. As she watched him, she moved toward the back of the store. So much pain filled her face when she looked at him, and so much long ago love, desire for younger years when they were still friends, still alive.

Circling around the opposite aisles, browsing, keeping one eye on her, I worked my way around to the back of the store.

She peered over the top of an end cap, watching Davis. She had no idea I stood beside her, her eyes glued only to him.

From the corner of my eye, I noted her innocent beauty, the long dark lashes contrasting and shielding the light blue eyes. The perky nose with its gentle slope, her clear complexion and full pink lips, I could see why Davis thought he loved her, not to mention why Franky did love her. Her inner beauty shined through to the surface of her outer beauty, a rare woman indeed.

"Can you see me?" Her honey voice dripped when she realized I stared in her direction.

I knew she was speaking to me. Maybe if I didn't answer, she wouldn't realize I was dead, too.

I didn't change my expression.

She turned to search out the window on her

other side, looking for people or architecture of interest, anything that would tell her that I was staring through her, not at her. I knew she would flee if I spoke up, answered her, so with her head turned, I reached over and grabbed her arm, hoping that if she disappeared, I would go where she did.

"Joanie, wait," I pleaded, just before we disappeared from the small store.

"Let go of me, please," she begged.

I viewed our new surroundings. Night had fallen already. The darkness hadn't impaired my vision, though. No street lights lined this barren street.

We stood in the middle of a black top road just wide enough for two cars. It hadn't been used in years. Weed filled cracks ran from one side to the other.

"I can't. I don't know where I am," I held tight to her arm.

"Ah, newly dead? I should have realized when I saw you with him that you were newly dead, not just another tourist.

"I remember those days. Of course, that was forty-nine years ago. So, you were staring at me in that store? Because of Davis?"

What could I tell her but the truth? I turned without letting go, first one way and then the other. There was nothing here, but I felt as though I knew where I was. "Yes. My name is Mel," I met her eyes. They were crystal clear, and flowed over with sadness, lost love. "I'm...uh...Davis' girlfriend."

I sighed, hoping she wouldn't twist away and leave me stranded here.

"Davis? His girlfriend? Oh!" She actually smiled. "So, he knows love now? Real love? Love like Franky and I used to have?"

"Yes, real love. He told me about you, about yours and Franky's love, about the baby."

The smile vanished from her face. "I never got to hold my baby. Unborn babies pass straight through, you know? I never even saw his face, my precious baby. I was so happy when I found out. Davis would have been his uncle. We were going to name him Davis." A tear slipped from the corner of her eye, rolling slowly down her cheek. "Will I ever be happy again?" She looked down the empty road we stood on, "This is where it all happened. Davis was supposed to win that race, go off to college. I would not see him again for a very long time. By the time he returned from college, Franky and I would have been an old married couple and probably have three children. I loved Franky so much, and I had grown to love Davis, too, as Franky's best friend. All I wanted to do was let him know that I loved him, that we loved him, me, Franky and Donna. I shouldn't have done it. I shouldn't have drawn that heart with my fingers. He's been so angry at me. It hurts so much, Franky laying there, Davis angry, Donna not my friend anymore. I'm so alone."

Her face turned to mine, and I embraced her, let her cry, became her friend. When I released her, I kept my hand on her arm.

"You can let go. I won't leave you stranded. Even if I did, or someone else did, you just have to think about where you want to go and you'll be there," a sad smile crossed her lips. "It's interesting, being dead, the things you can do that you never could before because of worldly restrictions." I let go of her. "Yes, if only I hadn't made that heart sign. I couldn't help myself. I wanted him to know how we felt as he crossed that last finish line, before he went away and maybe never returned." Her eyes met mine and she smiled. "How long have you known him? In all these years here, I didn't know he had someone else."

"All my life, it seems. He's the guy I dreamed I would meet after college, or in college, the one that would change my life and complete me," love filled my face.

"Aw, it shows. Does he feel the same way?"

"Yes, he does."

"I'm so happy for him. Franky and I had that once, that love. I need so much forgiveness," My hands sought her shoulders, turned her to me.

"Davis isn't angry with you. He used to be, at first, but not now," I shook my head. "He's been searching for you everywhere. He was looking for you at the school when he saw me."

Her brows rose with joy. "Really? So, I have done something good,"

"Yes, really, he's not angry with you. And you did the best thing in the world for me, sent him to me."

"Mel? When Davis saw me before he crossed the finish line, his face used to light up, like yours does when you say his name. Does that happen when he sees you?"

I couldn't believe I had to think about that, "I

don't know, but he radiates love when he looks at me."

"Oh, Franky used to look at me that way. Do you think he ever will again?"

"The way Davis talks about your love for each other, yes. I believe that no amount of time, pain, anger he has suffered in his life could keep him from looking at you like that when he finally joins us. He's just biding time until he can look at you like that again."

She took a few steps down the street, then off the road onto the shoulder. "I was standing right here that night, jumping up and down when I saw his car coming. Do you know what I did when I first saw it?" she missed her life, as much because Franky wasn't with her.

"No, I don't."

"I searched the crowd on the opposite side for my Franky, and when I found him, I blew him a kiss. Then when I turned back, and drew the heart to show Davis our love, he looked at the heart and smiled. Then that horribly loud sound of the front tire blowing, the screeching of metal, the flip of the car, Davis' body flying through the air," she lowered her head and shook it, brought a hand to her face.

I knew she was crying, again. My hand rested on her shoulder. "He would have won."

"Joanie, it was just an accident. It wasn't your fault, or anyone else's. You deserve to be happy."

Tears shone in her eyes when she turned to me. "You should have seen Franky at my funeral, Davis' funeral. His heart was broken in three."

"He loved you, Joanie. Go to him. He's almost ready to join us. He'll forgive you, too. Please, go back to him. Davis wants to see you, too. You can't live in the past and be happy, so live for the future you will have with Franky in eternity."

"I need to go someplace else first. You two should really go see Scotland. It's beautiful this time of year. Make him happy, Mel. Make our Davis happy," and then she was gone.

As Davis and I rolled on the hills of Scotland, following Joanie's advice, holding each other in the lush, long, flowing grasses, laughing, snuggling, I felt I was already in Heaven.

My heart filled with sorrow when I thought I might have to leave without Davis. I peered at the crystal clear sky above me, few puffy clouds floating slowly toward the sun, and wondered what it would be like, the other side.

"Your four months with me must be long over by now, Adonis," I teased sadly. I felt we had been together forever already.

"Don't think about Monday. Just think about now, here, us." He rolled up on his side and leaned over to kiss me—a long, tender, searching kiss.

I had taken for granted that I would still be alive, go to college, have children, live a life after school. He was right. I didn't want to take this time we had for granted by worrying about our future together. My hands sought his face, his hair, his warm, flushed neck.

"So she was going to see Franky? Donna?" he whispered into my hair.

"I don't know. I'm not sure. She just said she had somewhere else to go before she went to Franky. She's very worried after seeing him at her funeral, seeing the anger in your eyes, she's so alone, Davis. The look in her eyes when she spoke of Franky nearly broke my heart."

I ran my fingers through the hair on above his ears, traced the paths around them.

A moan crept up his throat, out his slightly opened lips. His eyelids fell for a moment.

"Yeah, it was really bad, the funerals. Franky was so broken at Joanie's, especially after going to mine and Donna's the day before."

"To lose so many friends in a single night, I know he had to be devastated."

"Mmhm."

"We can't live in the past."

"Nope." He rolled back to his back, searching the fluffy clouds above us. The grass cushioned my body from the hard earth below it, more comfortable than the lumpy mattress I slept on in life.

"Hey, that one looks like a bear! Look! Over there."

"Yes, it does. There's a lion!" I pointed to the south.

His head rolled to the side. I could feel his eyes on me as I watched the lion dissipate into two separate clouds. I turned to meet his gaze. The love shone on his face, through his smile, in his eyes, just as I had told Joanie it did. He was as glad that we had found each other, even in this life, as I was. We would never have met in the world we left behind. His hand squeezed mine and he rolled up on his elbow to kiss me again. This time, the clouds did not draw his attention from me, or mine from him.

All I would remember of Scotland would be the

comfortable cushioning of the rolling hills as we shared our love, and the fluffy clouds passing above us.

Fog drifted and settled eerily around our clasped hands in the streets of London. The chilly dampness affecting tourists around us did not affect us. I had completely shed the worldly binds that held me before. No pain, no chills, no worries, just love remained.

We scared lions from their hunt of a young lame giraffe in the Outback of Australia, knowing full well the poor injured giraffe would become pray elsewhere.

As light grew and faded from the earth, as we became bored before the Pyramids, Davis turned me toward him, "Maybe we should go back. You should say goodbye to your mother, your grandparents."

"Not yet."

In Central Park, we settled, and we had yet to hear any news.

The waters riffled with waves around Lady Liberty, and our hands never parted, our ghostly bodies always close, touching in some way.

No pictures to take as we toured the world, only memories of our travels with each other, memories of our love shared around the world.

As we tried to stretch our arms around a redwood tree with our hands held, Davis pulled me around it and back into his arms.

"Marry me."

What could I say to that? We were dead. We were in danger of being separated forever by fate. We would be lost to each other in the morning, unless…

"How could I say no to Adonis?" I smiled up at him.

Church to church we travelled in search of a wedding about to begin.

And we finally found one, near our hometown.

I went one way, Davis another, the only time we'd separated since we had found Joanie in Paris.

Locating the bride's room, bridesmaids fluttering about her, fixing her hair, makeup, dress, I waited. Her dress was beautiful, filled with lace, a dress I would have chosen myself. Nerves filled my stomach, realizing that I was about to have a wedding day, a dream wedding day that I had not had to plan or pay for, a wedding day with all of the happiness and none of the worry.

Slipping into the bride's gown with her caused her to shiver and complain of the cold in the church. I felt a tinge of guilt, making her cold on her most special of days, but it was my special day, too. I wanted to be beautiful for Davis, my Adonis, my eternal love.

It was an incredible old church. Stained glass filled each window, mahogany pews with deep red padding, a statue of Christ, arms welcoming, open wide, behind the lectern. I wasn't even aware what religion the church touted. I was only glad to be here.

As the chilled bride and I first stepped to the aisle, the bride's father serving as my own estranged one, I smiled broadly at Davis.

Davis waited between me and the reverend.

He looked stunning in the black tuxedo with the baby blue cummerbund and bowtie. The blue drew my eyes to his.

He smiled softly at me across the room, so handsome.

I glanced at the strangers' faces smiling up at the bride, at me, as I passed to the rhythm of the wedding march.

My mother, her face flushed with joy, sat in the very front pew. She was happier than I had ever seen her in life. How curious, I thought. She looked so proud, so... sober. No glaze filmed her eyes as she smiled at me. How was it that she was here?

The face of the man who walked me down the aisle was unfamiliar, because he did not belong to me, but he served as the father I never knew in life. He had a kind face, and it filled with a bittersweet glow as he looked upon the bride, upon me, for this moment his pride and joy.

I wondered if the cameras' flashing bulbs that brightened the candle lit church momentarily would later reveal the reason for the bride's now chattering teeth.

Well, I wouldn't discover the answer to that question, as I would be leaving in the morning. I giggled thinking about the possible reaction of the bride and groom as they viewed their wedding photos, filled with light balls here, ghosts there.

"What's so funny?" Davis asked over the reverend's introduction as he took my hand from my pretend father, traced his finger over my bare shoulder, leaned in to sneak a kiss.

"I was just thinking about our wedding photos," he chuckled in response. "Poor guy," he thumped his chest. "You are absolutely beautiful, my Aphrodite."

"And you are stunning, Adonis!"

We gazed into each other's eyes and said, "I do."

Davis kissed me deeply as we were pronounced husband and wife.

We posed for pictures we would never see, hoping they wouldn't be completely ruined by our presence.

We entered the reception hall, with the wedding party.

We drank champagne, after clinking our glasses, our arms entwined.

We cut the cake and carefully took the first bite.

We danced the first song as the bride and groom, twirling about the floor in a waltz that I never before had danced. The long, lacy, full dress made me feel like Cinderella, and my prince finally held me in his arms.

"I feel a little guilty," Davis whispered in my ear

as we danced.

"Why?" My love filled eyes found his and he kissed me again.

"Franky and Joanie. This poor bride and groom freezing."

"You don't think Franky would want this for you? We found it here, maybe they will, too," I offered.

We slipped from the bride and groom as they changed to leave for their honeymoon so they might enjoy their first night together without the chill we seemed to give them. Off they drove to some romantic, unknown destination.

Off we went to our romantic honeymoon destination, the park, our park, the park where we first kissed, the park with so much meaning to our lives and afterlives, the swings, the innocence of our wasted youth.

Lying on our backs in the soft grass, stars above us twinkling signals of joy in our basking love, Davis slid his arm from beneath my head. He took my hand and pulled me to my feet. "Come on."

"Is it time? Is he ready?"

"No. There's something you need to do, now, before it's too late."

Staring at the outside of the small white house where I had spent the past few years of my life surviving, studying, striving against my mother, I shivered at the thought of seeing her this last time, saying goodbye. Would she be better now? Was she really sober, as during our wedding? How had she been there, at the wedding? Was she there in her dreams?

Mother tossed in her restless sleep. Moans of regret inundated the blackened room. Davis looked upon her with pity, and then glanced at me, a silent plea.

In all my life, I never remembered my mother being happy. I only remembered the drinking. I only remembered not having a normal relationship with her, as my friends had enjoyed with their mothers. Shopping together, vacations in new destinations, her expressed joy at my achievements, those were all events I thought of now that I thought I should have had then.

How would my life have been different if I had had those times? Mother wouldn't have been drunk that day. I may not have died, but then, I would not have found love. I would not have found Davis across time in this other dimension. All situations happen for a reason, and perhaps the accident would have still happened. It was the argument that took her eyes from the road, not the drinking.

I watched her suffering in her sleep and searched the room for the empty bottle that had become a fixture on the bedside table in her room. The empty glass usually beside the bottle was not visible, and where it should have been, there was no bottle. Instead, a business card took their place, Alcoholics Anonymous. I glanced at Davis, a question filling my eyes, "She quit?"

He could only shrug in reply.

In spite of the life I had missed out on with her, she was still my mother, and she suffered now with the guilt of my death. I thought about her face in the first pew at the church where we shared the wedding of others, the proud smile she held for her daughter, the bride. A shiver passed through her as I rested my open palm on her forehead, stroked her dark hair, so much like mine, sent calmness, joy, love from my open heart, down my arm and into her dream filled sleep.

Without waking, she pulled the covers up around her neck and turned to her side.

She had been dreaming of the accident, my face as the dump truck whirled at us.

She dreamed of my urn on the mantel, the only part of me left to her except memories.

Davis reached over her bed and took my free hand. He smiled tenderly with his dazzling blue eyes into my pain-filled ones. I thought of our wedding, the cake, the dance, our travels around the world, but mostly our love for each other.

From my heart, down my left arm, and into my mother's sleeping mind passed these joyful love filled memories. In her dream she hugged me tightly, crying on my shoulder. She whispered near my face that she was so proud of me and that she loved me so much, as her tears fell to the pastel blue gown she wore, mother of the bride.

No trace of vodka wafted between us to ruin the mother daughter memory that I would take with me and that she would wake to.

I looked down at her, a tear falling for what could have been, and now was, and for the first time, I saw a smile upon her face, all trace of worry lines vanished, and I knew she would be okay.

How beautiful and young she appeared with just a smile. No more worry, no more drinking, no more guilt, just a tender smile brightening her features.

"Good bye, Mom," I whispered, planting a wispy kiss upon her trembling forehead.

Chattering teeth paused as in her dream state she replied, "Good bye, Amelia. I'm so happy for you. You've found what I never seemed to be able to find, what I never had with your father, or anyone. You've found love. Always remember, no matter where you are that I love you."

I moved around the bed and into Davis' arms as the tears flowed from my eyes.

And too soon, I would have to say good-bye to him.

It wasn't fair.

Life hadn't been fair.

Now, afterlife was not fair, either.

38

$\mathcal{M}other$ resting peacefully, we returned to the park, the swings creaking to us in the breeze. Silence followed us, until two tiny voices echoed into our night world. We searched the park, chasing the happy childlike voices, always just out of reach. Our smiles grew as we located the source.

Two small children played in the park, a boy and a girl. Much too young to be left alone, they roused my curiosity. They were adorable children, but their tattered clothes bore holes and hung loosely upon their too thin frames. They looked homeless, the poor darlings.

"Davis?" my hand squeezed his in concern.

"I don't know," he answered without my asking.

"Can they see us?"

Two little round faces, cheeks pink with laughter beneath dirty handprints, pulled at grass, clutched handfuls of gravel, chased each other, and tumbled down the hill.

"Are they . . ."

Davis shrugged. "They shouldn't be out this late. They must be ghosts."

No, they were too young! Horrible thoughts filled my mind about how they arrived here.

We followed, watching them from the rise as they played among the child toys there.

They were so cute, so happy to be so destitute.

The little girl, who seemed to be about two, tumbled over, scraping her knee on the sidewalk. Her wail filled the night air, "Owwwwwwwy!"

Her brother ran to her side, putting his arm about her, comforting her. With his help, she rose and they hobbled back up the hill toward us.

"Can you help us find our Maryann?" the little boy scowled.

"Poor babies," my brows furrowed at Davis.

They were dead, and like me when it first happened, they didn't know.

"Who's Maryann?" Davis fell to his knees and inquired. Already I could tell he would have made a terrific dad, uncle, grandfather.

"The woman we live with. She left us over there," he pointed, the highway filled with the headlights of wee hour travelers. Red and blue lights flashed in one section, the scream of sirens piercing the night.

"By those cars? Those lights?" Now it was Davis' turn to frown.

"Yes, she stopped the car and put us out. She was mad because Wiley was crying because she was hungry. Maryann yelled at her, 'If you don't stop making that terrible noise, I'll pull over right here and put you out on the street!' Wiley's not hungry anymore, are you, Wiley?"

"No," the little girl shook her head, her bottom lip poked out. Her curly blonde hair bounced with the action and her eyes brightened with tears.

I dropped to my knees, searching their faces. "Was Maryann your mother?" I had to ask. I had thought mine unhappy, cruel, but this woman, to put these babies out like that, she must have been insane.

"No, we don't have a mother. We don't have a father, too. We just stayed with Maryann. She promised those people she would take care of us. We kept getting sick, and she couldn't work, and then, she lost her job. She was taking us with her to find another job. We made her angry. She put us out there," the boy pointed again, saw the police and ambulance lights, and became excited. "Policemen, policemen! Can we go see them? Can we ride in their car?" He turned his eyes to me, and I turned mine to Davis.

"Not right now, buddy. Maybe another time."

Like the statue in the church, behind the pulpit at our wedding, I spread my arms to them. Wiley limped into me and let go of her knee long enough to circle my neck with her tiny arms. Her brother soon followed and I wrapped my arms protectively around them.

"Swing?" Wiley pointed over my shoulder. I nodded, "Sure," and picked her up. Davis reached down for the little boy's hand. "What's your name, kid?"

"Franky. I'm the oldest," his red head bobbed responsibly. Davis stopped mid-step. I turned, still holding little Wiley in my arms.

"What a coincidence," Davis reasoned.

We pushed the children on the swings, treating them as we might our own. Curiosity led us to the list. We couldn't see leaving them on their own to find their own way. Who would watch out for them if we were scheduled to leave in the morning? They'd had such sad little lives, and now here they were. They surely wouldn't be buried, as there was nobody to bury them. Would they ever know they were dead, or had their lives already been dead to them? Did they need to know they were dead?

I wondered if there was adoption in this... place, where we were now, or perhaps afterward.

Wiley slept in my arms; Franky slumped over Davis' shoulder.

Yes, he would have made a terrific dad!

I smiled at my husband in this other realm.

"Ah, what adorable little ones," a kindly old lady at the end of the line on our right smiled.

"We found them wandering in the park, alone," I sent a knowing look her way.

"How tragic. Here, take these clothes for them. Make their days here special, not like paupers. I was taking those to my own grandchildren, they passed before me. Made them myself. They'll fit perfectly, I'm sure."

I sent a curious look her way, but she turned and vanished into the white wall, the clothes lying over my arm.

One glimpse of the list told us the children would not go through alone.

Below my name, now written, Amelia Kern Wilburn, were the names Franky Wilburn and Wiley Wilburn. But still, no Davis. As if by wishing for adoption brought it about, the children had become ours. I closed my eyes and wished to see Davis' name there. When I opened them, nothing had changed.

Outside the brightness around the list, I changed the children while they slept. I ran my fingers through Wiley's soft curls, and pressed down Franky's red ones as best I could.

"Let's go," Davis smiled sadly at me.

"Oh, Davis, what's happening? Why is this happening? These poor children…"

"These poor children who look too cute in those clothes! That frilly pink dress makes Wiley look happy. And Franky, there, what a charmer, hey?" he grinned.

"Yeah, just like his Greek god father! But why? Why did we find them? Why did that happen to them?"

"I guess somebody, somewhere, is giving us a little bit of a future, our wedding, these children. Don't you think it's funny, this boy's name? I'm sure had I lived and married, I would have named my son after Franky. He was my best friend. He would have been my best man at my wedding. Of course, then I wouldn't have you, and now that I do, I wouldn't have it any other way. This past week... the first time I saw you, I knew we were meant to be together."

He rested his free arm over my shoulder and led his family to the only place he could take them.

DAVIS

In a spare room of the old Victorian house we lay the children on a big, soft bed. I planted a kiss on both foreheads, their new clothes clean and bright in the darkness.

"What's this?" Donna whispered at my side. "A niece and nephew? You two work fast!" her hand tapped my arm. I told her the story of their arrival, in the park, the mystery that had been their lives.

When I finished, her face dawned a tender smile as Mel stroked Wiley's blonde head gently. "So, a trip around the world, a wedding, which by the way sounds like a blast, and two kids later, I get to do my aunty duties and babysit? Did you find her, Joanie?"

"Yes, we found her in Paris. Mel grabbed her arm and ended up out at Tillers Road. She told Joanie everything was fine, we weren't angry. We thought she was coming here. You haven't seen her?" I cast a concerned look in Mel's direction.

"No, she hasn't shown up, yet," Donna searched first my face, then Mel's.

"She said she had someplace to go first," Mel added.

"Where?" Donna and I asked in unison.

"She didn't elaborate, just someplace."

MEL

Here we were, near the end, and no Joanie, neither Donna nor Davis could think where she could have gone.

"Let's not worry. She'll turn up, hopefully. She's suffered for a long time."

DAVIS

"Oh, if you could have seen the look in her eyes, heard her tears falling when she recalled the past!" Mel shook her head.

Donna and I glanced at her, then back at each other.

"We need to find her," I told Donna.

"I'll call her while I'm here. I'll talk to her, see if I can get her to come here," my sister's sad smile made me glance at Franky.

"It would be nice, all of us together again at the end," I nodded hopefully.

"Go on you two, see if you can talk Franky into giving it up. If my fingers could've grasped the pillow, it would already be over," Donna winked.

"It wasn't meant to be that way. I think Joanie's supposed to be here."

I squeezed my sister's shoulder. She looked older, wiser, not the nineteen-year-old girl I left here earlier. Her green eyes sparkled lovingly at Franky and Wiley. "Hey, another Red?" She nodded at the little boy sleeping there.

"Yeah," I took Mel's hand and we moved to my old friend's room.

A young woman rested in a high back chair, snoring lightly, Franky's niece, a paperback romance opened and turned cover up on her lap.

Franky's breaths came more shallowly than before, further apart. "I think it's getting close. Sometimes, you can talk to the almost dead, their souls are ready to hear you, then. They even answer, I hear. I've never seen it. I know Franky can hear me, he groans when I speak to him, but he's never been close enough to speak to me. I hope he speaks to me now."

MEL

"Me, too." I smiled sweetly at Franky's niece

while Davis spoke to him. Franky did have family who cared and I was glad he hadn't spent his entire life completely alone as I had thought the first time I came here with Davis.

"Hello, my old friend. I missed you at the wedding, our wedding," Davis began as I placed my hand on Franky's forehead like I had my mother's, and I remembered our wedding in the beautiful church across town, right down to the shivering bride and groom, the unseen wedding photos.

Franky dreamed of nothing, though I sent him all of my thoughts. His eyelids flickered; he released a slight groan.

"You didn't get to dance with my lovely bride, Franky. You're going to be upset about that. She's gorgeous, even after two children."

I rolled my eyes at Davis and shook my head, but I thought of little Wiley and Franky, tucked away in that spacious bed in the room down the hall, their Aunt Donna looking after them like they were her own. The image flowed from my mind, down my arm, into Franky's head.

* * *

DAVIS

"Yep, just like I told you, I named my boy after you.

"You know, Franky, Mel leaves in a few hours with the children. I sure would like to leave with her, but I can't do that, unless you forgive me. Are you close old friend? I lived my life without her; I don't want to live my eternity without her, too.

"I'm sorry I screwed up not checking my tire, Franky. I'm sorry, what happened to Joanie. Please, Franky, forgive me."

Mel took her hand from his cooling, perfectly still forehead to wipe away my tears. No chattering teeth, no shivering limbs, he was so close, but still no answer.

We stood silent waiting as he breathed, in, out, slower, slower, and then from his barely parted lips one word flowed, "Joanie," barely a whisper.

The young woman in the chair snapped awake instantly, hearing the slightest noises.

"Ben!" she called down the hallway. "Ben, come

quick! He's waking up!"

We stood clear as the nephew we had seen on our second visit rushed into the room.

"What? What did he say?"

Franky's dry lips worked to form the word again, "Joanie," he forced the name free.

"Oh," the nephew sighed. "He's talking about the love of his life. She died in some freak car accident at a drag race back in the 60s. Uncle Franky was only 19, but he asked her to marry him. They were gonna have a baby. It's a sad story. Did he ever tell you that story?" a pause, a head shake, "He used to tell me all of the time. I can't help but think how much happier he would have been if she were still here.

"You know, that's why he never married. Her death broke his heart. Well, hers and two other friends, his best friend, died the same night."

MEL

A tear fell from Davis' eyes as he listened to his

story, told from the lips of Franky's relative. "Not quite the story you expected to pass down to your family," Davis whispered to his old friend.

"Joanie," the ancient voice crackled again, much louder.

"Even on his death bed, he waits for her, calls for her," Ben stroked the old man's hand. "I hope she makes it to greet you, Uncle."

"It's almost time," a voice whispered to my left. I turned to smile at her, glad she was here.

"Joanie!" Davis' eyes grew wide with joy. "You're here! Joanie, I'm sorry... I..."

"Shh!" She quieted his apology. "Of course I'm here. There's a crazy red head in the other room calling me, and the love of my life needs me!" She moved around me, hugged Davis, and stood near Franky's head. "Never you mind apologies and all that. We can't live in the past, Davis." She reached up and patted his cheek. "I'm here my love. I'm here and I want to take you home with me if you'll go." She kissed Franky's dry lips, his cheek, his forehead.

"Joanie..." The name more clear now, followed by the faintest trace of a smile

"We'll leave you two alone. Mel will be leaving

soon." Davis squeezed Joanie again.

"Hopefully, we'll all be leaving. It's been a long forty-nine years."

We returned to our sleeping angels. Donna hugged Mel, and then picked up Wiley, squeezing her, kissing her pink porcelain like cheek. Franky rubbed his eyes. "Is it time to go, Daddy?"

Davis' eyes caught mine. "Yes, son, it is. Come on!" Donna gave little Franky a squeeze and a peck on the cheek that made him wrinkle his nose and wipe his cheek with his hand. "Yuck!" He remarked as Davis swung him over his shoulder.

"I'll keep trying," Donna patted her brother's arm.

"No need. Joanie's in there with Franky right now. She'll probably be glad for some company in a few minutes."

"Oh, Davis, finally! Maybe now…"

"Yeah, maybe. He's still hanging in there, though. It would be nice if we could all go home together."

The sun fought its way over the horizon, sending slivers of light into the black room through the edges of the blinds.

"Oh, Davis, I can't leave without you."

"You don't have a choice. If you don't go right when you're scheduled, you'll only be able to go left later, and then none of this will have existed to you. You and I won't have existed."

Solemnly we left the gloomy house. We had so little time left to spend together. Wiley awakened in my arms, a smile breaking her round, rosy-cheeked face.

"Swing, Mommy?" her sweet voice requested.

"Not right now, honey."

"Okay," she wanted down to chase her bother in circles around Davis and I, her bare feet patting the ground, as we walked hand in hand. In a few moments, she returned, putting one of her hands on my hand and the other hand on Davis' hand and pulling, broke our connection. We laughed as she held each of our hands, pulled downward and hopping, lifting her feet off the ground.

"Swing? Swing? Swing?"

We held her hands in ours and lifted her off the ground with each step we took, swinging her in front of us, and then behind us. Her laughter pierced the morning breeze. Little Franky ran under her when she flew before us, and then around us and under her again when she flew behind. They were so different than when we first saw them last night. As if love had been all they needed to fill out their happy faces and make their clothes fit perfectly.

I was so different than when Davis first saw me. I had died at eighteen, but I felt I had aged five years, so much wiser than when I had entered this strange world.

And Davis had changed since I saw him in the school that first day that I had tried to return to normal after the accident. He seemed older, too, but much more handsome than our first encounter.

"Davis, I don't know what I would have done if you hadn't been in the school that day, if I hadn't seen you."

He searched the blue sky before us. "So, you're telling me that you're not so smart that you would have figured out what happened to you if you continued going to school, hanging with your friends? You couldn't have figured it out without your incredibly handsome Adonis?"

I rolled my eyes to him again. "I guess I would have figured it out eventually, but I'm glad that I had your help. I'm glad that we had this time in this realm to fall in love. I'm glad I fell in love with a ghost," I rose to my tiptoes and kissed his cheek. The whiteness wavered before us and Wiley and Franky ran toward it in joy. "Time to go! Time to go!" Wiley chanted in her tiny voice.

The smile fell from my lips. I looked up at Davis.

He enveloped me, for the last time, kissed me hard and wiped the tears from cheeks with his thumbs.

"I'll always love you, Mel. I'm going to try to always remember you. When I do get to leave here, I'll look fruitlessly for you among the stars, forever if I have to. I won't have anything else more important to do than that. I'll treasure our love like no other has been treasured. As I roam the hallways of the school, walk the streets by your house, dawn the stores of the mall, wherever I go, you'll be with me."

Tears pooled his eyes as his mouth fell to mine again.

"Come on, Mommy! Come on, Daddy!" Little Franky took our hands and pulled.

"We're coming, honey," I assured him.

One person stood between us and the bright wall before us. He looked around nervously searching, but never looked back. Thankfully, we couldn't go through until he did and apparently, his time wasn't just then.

Davis held us as we waited, a family hug. Our time together was nearing the end, and the man before us still had not passed through.

I was happy. The more time I could spend in Davis' arms, the better. His embrace filled me with so much love that I knew it would last all of eternity, if needed.

"When are we going, Daddy?" little Franky impatiently asked.

"Daddy's not going, son. But you and Mommy will go soon."

"Why aren't you coming with us, Daddy?"

"Uh... well..." The man before us peered at the white wall, smiled, and vanished as he stepped through. Just like that, it was our turn.

I didn't want to let go of Davis.

I didn't want to go without him.

This had to be the most difficult time in my life, more difficult than discovering I was dead, more difficult than living with my mother.

I loved him so deeply.

"Mel?" he tilted my damp chin so he could look

at me. "I love you."

"Oh, Davis, I can't say good bye! I can't!"

"Just tell me you love me and step through."

"No! No, I won't! I can't! Come with us. Just come!"

"You can do it. You will. I'll find you, somehow; I'll find you. Now tell me you love me and go."

"No. I don't understand why you can't go with us. It wasn't your fault! It was an accident. A stupid accident. There's no blame, no forgiveness to wait for. Come with us!"

The children pressed closer to the wall as Davis led me after them.

"I can't, Mel; I've tried before. Maybe you're right. Maybe it wasn't my fault. But nothing's changed." As if on cue, we faced the list, his name still absent. "Now! Tell me, Mel."

I looked up at him, my face soaked with tears, my heart splitting in two.

"I love you, Davis. I'll always love you..." I choked out.

"Mommy! Mommy!" Franky tugged at my shirt.

"I'm coming, sweetie," I assured him, my eyes never leaving the livid blue of Davis'.

"Is Aunt Donna coming, too?" He tugged on my

shirttail.

"No, son," Davis answered, his eyes never leaving mine.

"Then is she here to say good bye? Who's that man with her? And that woman?"

Hope gleamed in Davis' face transferring to mine as we turned.

"Davis, old buddy! What's this about a wedding? Hey, is that the little rascal, my namesake?" The young man tousled Franky's red hair.

"Hey, Red! Another, Red!" He teased Donna.

"Shut up, Jerkface!" Donna slugged him in the arm.

"Ouch, careful there, Red!"

"Franky," Davis whispered, again.

"Man! Glad I didn't miss meeting you!" He eyed Mel, sending his flirty wink her way. "She's a foxy chick, Davis!" He punched Davis playfully in the stomach.

"Franky," Davis repeated.

"What's wrong with you, man? You act like you're seein' a ghost or something! Knock it off, will ya'? You're holdin' up the line, there. The train's a waiting and we're all gettin' on board.

Can't leave this great looking bunch hanging now, can you? See ya' on the other side, man!"

"So, we're okay? You and me?"

"Davis, man, you were always kinda thick in the head. It was never about you and me. It was about you and her. It was about you forgiving yourself. Forgiveness comes from here," he touched his heart. "You guys have been waitin' around for forty-nine years for nothin'! You could have went on. It was never about me. It was about her..." he poked a thumb at Donna, "and her," he poked his other thumb at Joanie, "forgiving themselves. You could have went on without us. You didn't have to hang around here, but you did it for her," he smiled at his best friend, nodded toward me.

"Hm," Davis thought, "I think you're wrong, Franky. It was about you!" Davis looked around at all of us, old friends and new. "If you and Joanie weren't here, our family wouldn't be complete, old friend." He rested his hand on Franky's shoulder and Franky placed his hand over Davis'.

"Ah, you're gettin' all mushy!" He pushed Davis away. "Now, you two," he waved a finger at us, "have an eternity to live. We'll be right behind you!" Franky winked at me. I couldn't help but smile back at him. He was such a character, such a flirt. I could see why he and Davis were best friends.

"I can't go, man, unless I'm on the list. I'm not there. Donna's not there, man. Look!" Davis pointed to the list, turning slowly in the center of the whiteness surrounding us.

"What are you talking about man? You've always been there. If you don't leave now, you'll miss your shot. Go!"

Davis and I turned toward the list. Donna ran to it. As sure as Franky's words, all of our names were there: Donna Wilburn, Davis, Amelia, Franky and Wiley Wilburn. And just below our names were Franky's and Joanie's.

The joy radiating from Davis' face filled the room. Donna whooped. Davis hugged his old friend, again and then rested his arm across my shoulders. "Come on, kids! We're going home!"

As the five of us pressed through the white wall, his lips met mine for the very last time, in this realm.

Enjoy this sneak preview of my upcoming novel.

The

Hummingbird God

1

$\mathcal{I}$ saw the old, witch woman in the woods.

It was a cliche setting.

Really it was.

How many scary movies begin with some old witch in the woods?

Her long, salt and pepper hair hung past her butt, jutting out over her shoulders in a snarly, tangled mess of dull wire. Planted on her crown was a tattered fishing hat hosting not lures and hooks, but some strange objects I couldn't identify from a distance. She was reaching up, her gnarled, crooked, arthritic fingers bent every which way. I wondered how she could even complete her task with hands like that. A worn, black coat hung on her thin frame down to her ankles. She hadn't noticed me, or at least hadn't acted like she'd noticed me, until I was within her personal space—I was bad about that, getting into a person's personal space, even when ignoring my intuition. After one glance toward me with her rheumy eyes, she continued her work, unbothered by the fact that I watched her so closely.

I should have known when my stomach did that flip.

I should have left her to work and returned home, setting aside my pressing curiosity.

I'd had another argument with my mother, though and—after slamming the back door—ventured off into the woods behind our house to cool down. I guess I walked farther than I'd planned, which tells you how angry I was at her. I could have turned around, humbled myself for an apology, though it would have been fake because Mother was wrong this time. I could have been in my room, but curiosity and compassion became my doom.

I never returned to my room, my home, my mother.

I can't say I've been completely unhappy, because I've found more joy than I ever imagined!

I can't say that I miss my old life entirely, because I found what mother and I argued over the day I left.

Though I've been happier than I would have ever expected, I am imprisoned and now may never break free, but why would my mind feel I needed to?

I may never have a life of simplicity and normalcy.

I may never have the love of my life, the one I desire anyway.

Well, that is unless I decide, or he decides, that love is worth the risk of leaving here.

When I think about the old woman in the woods, I see her as if five minutes have passed since I entered her personal space and asked the simple question, "Would you like some help with that?"

A croaky, harsh chuckle traveled up her throat and escaped her lips before she replied, "Are you sure you want to help?"

"Yes, of course, if you need help. I don't want to offend you."

It was so easy for me to say that simple three letter word then, and now it seems the most difficult word in the English language to pronounce.

* * *

"Alrighty!" Her voice crackled, "Take this jug and fill those." With a sweep of her hand she indicated upside down bottles hanging in the high branches of the trees around us. "It's getting more difficult for me to climb these days."

"What is this?" I took the jug from her hand, a clear, light brown liquid sloshing about inside. I thought it was alcohol.

"Natural sugar water."

"Excuse me? Did you say sugar water?"

"No!" her voice became harsh, "I said natural sugar water! And don't think it anything else!" she turned on me violently. "You heard me the first time! Stop acting stupid, girl! Now, you asked to help, so climb that tree and fill that bottle!"

"Uh... uhm..." Fear knocked at my heart. I wanted to run, but I trembled my way up the tree, with one arm holding the jug. I didn't have to climb the tree the normal way. Someone had driven spikes into it for footholds, and as the tree grew, more spikes were added. At the top, an arm's length from the trunk, hung the bottles. I sat in the tree, lifted a bottle from its hook, and found it screwed into a round cap of some sort, about three inches in diameter, with several tiny holes on its surface, a circular ring around the outside of the cap. "What is this thing?" I called down to the scary, old woman below me.

"Don't you know anything? It's a hummingbird feeder! Again, you act stupid! You cannot help if you are going to be stupid! Stupid will get you in trouble! Stupid will get you exactly ..."

I balanced the round cap on the branch and began filling the bottle, but paused when her words dropped off. Her head flipped sideways, as if receiving a blow from the air. I thought it a tic, some disease crippling her muscles. I knew a little about that.

"Look lady, I just offered to help you. You don't have to be rude. I've never fed a hummingbird before, but I am very smart! I know hummingbirds might be tiny, little birds, but they fly so fast it's hard to see them sometimes. I can learn more, though." I shook my head and finished filling the bottle, replaced it to its perch, and moved down two spikes.

"Oh, you can see them," she whispered. "And they are hungry, greedy, mean little birds. I must keep these jugs filled at all times."

"All times? Don't birds migrate?" I perched on another branch, removing another feeder.

"Of course they do, stupid girl! But these feeders have to be maintained at all times or..." her head whipped to the side again, "We don't get many freezes here. Some of them remain, the older, crotchety ones."

"Uh, I know we don't get freezes often. That's the blight of Texas." I climbed back down the spikes, pausing before going up another tree, "Are you okay?" Tilting my head, and leaning to my right a little didn't provide much of a view of her face. Her hair hung around it and she humbly peered down at her feet as if chastised.

"I'm fine!" The abrupt yell forced me into action. "Just fill the feeders!"

"Okay... okay!" I couldn't wait to get out of there, away from her. She was a horribly bitter person. It was like she didn't enjoy feeding the hummingbirds. If she didn't like doing it, then why do it? I thought hummingbirds were beautiful, delicate creatures. To her, they seemed to be monsters, so why was she doing this? I glanced back down at her. Compared to her, Mom was a cuddly little puppy. This experience would definitely teach me to think before asking to help anyone. "There's only enough left for this feeder, and there's at least..." I did a quick count, "ten more."

"Oh, don't you worry about that. There's plenty more. I'll show you where to fill it when you're finished with that one."

As promised, she led me into the woods a little farther, and there before an old shack, stood a well. A round cover had been placed over the well, and she easily lifted it by a handle from the unhinged side.

Taking the jug from my hand, she hooked it onto the rope and turned the crank until I could no longer see the jug, only the descending rope. Her arthritic fingers jutted out around the handle and she pushed at it with only her palm.Â

As mean as she was, I felt sorry for her, "Would you like me to do that for you?"

"Fine!" she grumbled.

I took over the cranking, the heavy glass jug making it easy to lower. "May I ask you how old you are?"

"You wouldn't believe me if I told you."

I heard a splash below. "Let it go," she said, "wait. I count to 100 and it's full when I pull it up. It'll be heavy!" that deep throated chuckle.

Ugh! It made my spine crawl.

"Why wouldn't I believe you? What, are you like

a hundred?"

"Ha! A hundred? Do I look it, then?" her watery, crusty-cornered eyes peered around the well frame at me.

Uh, yeah! I thought, easily. She was starting to creep me out.

"I suppose I should thank you. Ha!"

"Uhm... okay. Never mind." I just wanted to finish the task I volunteered for and leave. The tiny hairs on the back of my neck flickered.

"Go on, then. Pull it up."

She was right. It was quite a bit heavier coming up. I put both hands on the handle and reeled. "Where's the sugar? I suppose in that shack? Can you bring some out?"

"Sugar! Ha!" she cackled, "Stupid, girl!" her head shook back and forth in frustration.

"Stop calling me that! I'm not stupid!" anger made me turn the crank faster. When the jug reached the opening, she pulled it to the side of the well and disconnected the rope. The water was brown.

"Yuck! Are you trying to poison those birds?" I was appalled by the site of it.

"Pfff! I wish! Now come on, finish up!"

Did she say I wish? She wanted to poison them? I need to get away from her, I told myself, eager to finish the job.

"Aren't you going to add sugar? You're just giving them this nasty, brown water?" I followed her back to the trees.

"Does it look the same as the other water?"

I peeked around her at the jug. "Yes." I nodded, a bit surprised that I hadn't noticed the color of the water earlier.

"What did I tell you the other was?"

"Sugar water!" I answered, a desire to please her brought a lilt of approval to my voice.

"No! Stupid girl! That's not what I said!" Her biting retort brought an involuntary wince.

Downtrodden, I thought a minute, certain she had said sugar water. "Natural sugar water?" I questioned.

"Ah, not so stupid girl, that is correct." She was sprite for her age and I had a hard time keeping up with her steps. I ran to catch up and reached for the jug. "Seriously? Out of that well? Let me taste it!"

She pulled the jug away, cradled it in one arm and slapped at my greedy hands with her free one.

"Never! Never, never, never should you taste this natural sugar water! It is for the birds only! Got it, stupid girl?"

Hmm, back to that again. "Okay, alright, I won't drink it. It's just... It's hard to believe there's natural sugar water in that well. I mean, how's..." I cut the question off. There was no need to hear that I was stupid, again.

I didn't need the answer. I was going to help her and be done with her. I would never return.

Three more trips to the well, alone, and I had finished the job. It was nearly dark by then and I was hungry, tired and eager to return home.

"Well, that does it. I think I'll go home, now."

"No! You can't leave!" She cast a stern look my way, followed by the head turning jerk with which I had become familiar. Her eyes humbled, searching the ground at her feet. "You must be starved. I will get you some dinner and you will behold the fruits of your labor."

"Fruits of my labor? Seriously?" Nobody talks like that anymore. She scurried off to the shack, leaving me to stand among the trees; I glanced up, the multitude of feeders forming a perfect circle around me. The light from the falling rays of sun glinted on the bottles, colorful prisms forming, rays dancing as the bottles moved with the slight breeze. Mesmerized by the jewel-like show it created, I took a seat on one of two tree stumps jutting from the ground, a perfect seat for nature's show. I watched the lights as the bottles and tree limbs moved in time.

"Here!" The old woman shoved a sandwich my way, and then a bottle of pop. I looked at the sandwich, pulling the bread apart. Peanut butter and honey, I could handle that. I hoped I wouldn't have to hear how stupid I was for being a vegetarian. "What? You think I'm stupid? I know you don't eat meat. He wouldn't choose..."

Slap! The noise seemed to come out of thin air. Her head whipped to the side, then her eyes dropped to the ground. "Eat!" The old lady ordered with a jerk of her head.

This woman was definitely weird. I was afraid to eat the sandwich now. I wrapped it back up and rose from the stump. "I think I'll eat it on the way home. I really need to be going now. My mother will be—"

"Wait! Look!" she pointed upward, drawing my attention back to the bottles above.

My eyes followed her crooked finger landing on the most amazing sight I had ever seen.

Hundreds, if not thousands, of tiny birds filled circles around the feeders, landing, drinking, flying away, repeating the process. As I stood there, one tiny, red-throated bird hovered before my eyes, circled my head three times, and returned to hover before me at eye level. It was magical, beautiful, and heartwarming. He zipped away, then rose to the trees to perch near a bottle.

"Sit, watch, and eat your sandwich."

"Okay." There was so much peace in watching the tiny birds that I hardly tasted the sandwich or the root beer.

Through the enchantment of the flight, the feeding, the singing, from another realm I heard her speaking, "I am two hundred and ninety-nine years, eleven months, twenty-nine days, twenty-three hours and forty-nine minutes old. I will be gone before the new hour. You will maintain the feeders from this day forward.

"There's one rule, and one rule only. Remember it: you must not drink the water from the well. Oh, and you may never leave here. He will not allow it, for the feeders must remain full. Your life is now here."

A distant voice, a dreamlike chant, drooping eyes, and when the birds disappeared at nightfall, the natural sugar water was gone, as well as the old woman whose translucent image wavered as my eyelids closed.

My fifth grade class voted me most likely to be the first woman president of the United States.

My parents expected me to play piano for the New York Philharmonic.

My grandmother thought I would be a star vocalist.

I didn't want any of that. Those were always their dreams for me.

All I ever wanted was to be who I was meant to be.

All I want now is him.

Look for this novel and all new releases at https://pgshriver.com

Thank you for reading my novel, *Delaying Eternity*. Would you do me a huge favor and post a review of this book on the site of purchase and on my Facebook page? Reviews are greatly appreciated by authors and readers alike. Thanks, again! Have a love filled day!

https://www.facebook.com/AuthorPGShriver

$\mathcal{B}orn$ in California, and raised in Minnesota and Texas, P.G. spent her early years writing poetry and winning poetry contests, while escaping the drama of childhood by reading great books.

P.G. sought an education at the University of Texas, where English, literature, and Education became interests. During the entire process of earning a BA and M. Ed writing never stopped and getting published became a greater goal.

P.G. graduated college and began a career in education. Currently, P.G. has retired from teaching after two rear end car accidents rendered her physically, mentally, and emotionally incapable of handling the stress and demands associated with teaching.

Delaying Eternity is P.G.'s first young adult romance novel in the realm of paranormal characters. *Delaying Eternity* was written during National Novel Writing Month for the Amazon Breakthrough Novel Award contest. The idea for the novel spawned from the loss of her cousin's eleven year old daughter. As most people do, the usual thoughts about events of teen years that her young cousin would never experience dwelled in Shriver's mind for a long time and eventually became the basis for *Delaying Eternity*.

9 781952 726323